mismatch

Also by lensey Namioka

Half and Half

An Ocean Apart, a World Away

Ties That Bind, Ties That Break

Yang the Youngest and His Terrible Ear

Yang the Third and Her Impossible Family

Yang the Second and Her Secret Admirers

Yang the Eldest and His Odd Jobs

mis

match

a novel by
**lensey
Namioka**

delacorte press

Published by
Delacorte Press
an imprint of
Random House Children's Books
a division of Random House, Inc.
New York

Visit us on the Web! www.randomhouse.com/teens
Educators and librarians, for a variety of teaching tools, visit us at
www.randomhouse.com/teachers

Library of Congress Cataloging-in-Publication Data
Namioka, Lensey.
Mismatch / Lensey Namioka.
p. cm.
Summary: Their families clash when a Japanese-American teenaged boy
starts dating a Chinese-American teenaged girl.
ISBN 0-385-73183-3 (trade) — ISBN 0-385-90220-4 (glb)
1. Chinese Americans—Juvenile fiction. 2. Japanese Americans—Juvenile
fiction. [1. Chinese Americans—Fiction. 2. Japanese Americans—Fiction.
3. Family life—Fiction. 4. Dating (Social customs)—Fiction. 5. High
schools—Fiction. 6. Schools—Fiction.] I. Title.
PZ7.N1426Mis 2006
[Fic]—dc22   2005003669

The text of this book is set in 12-point Baskerville BE Regular.

Book design by Angela Carlino

Printed in the United States of America

February 2006

10 9 8 7 6 5 4 3 2 1

BVG

For Saburo Namioka

as she headed toward the auditorium, Suzanne Hua knew she would nail her audition with the Lakeview High School Orchestra. She had been one of the best viola players in the orchestra at her old school. She had decided to audition at Lakeview because her sister, Rochelle, thought it would be a good way to meet some cool people. Sue didn't make friends easily, so any opportunity to meet other kids who loved music seemed worth a try.

As soon as Sue slipped inside the doors, she was entranced by the music coming from a violinist playing on the stage. Sue looked up at him, curious to see who could create such a beautiful sound, and saw that he was Asian American, like her. He had a slim build but wide shoulders, and he moved in a relaxed, sexy way. When he finished the passage with a brilliant run, Sue could feel her heart beating in time with the music.

"He's something, isn't he?" asked Mia, a girl Sue recognized from some of her classes. Mia sat in the second row, probably waiting for her own audition. "I think he just got one of the solo parts in a double concerto."

Mr. Baxter, the Lakeview conductor, walked over to the violinist, and from the way they were nodding and smiling, Sue guessed that Mia was right.

Before she could learn more, Mr. Baxter called Mia's name.

"Wish me luck," said Mia. "I play clarinet in the band, but I want to try out for the orchestra because they might go to Tokyo this year."

Tokyo! Sue managed to smile and wish Mia luck, but her heart thumped against her ribs. She groped her way to a seat and sat down, repeating the name *Tokyo* over and over again in her head. Tokyo might be a fun vacation for Mia, but for Sue, it presented a world of problems. What would her mother say? Maybe Sue shouldn't even audition? *Wait.* Mia had said the orchestra was only *hoping* to make the trip. *Why worry before I need to?* Besides, there were so many other things to think about . . . like that cute violinist, for one.

Mia played pretty well, and when she finished, Mr. Baxter gave her a thumbs-up sign. Mia jumped off the stage and waved her clarinet as she passed Sue. "Hey, I made third chair! Good luck on your audition!"

Sue smiled and waved back just as Mr. Baxter called her name. She walked up to the stage, tuned her viola quickly, opened her score, and breezed through her audition piece, the way she'd known she would.

"Good work, Suzanne," said Mr. Baxter. "I'm putting you in the second row of the viola section for now. But I'm pretty sure you'll be moving up soon."

Sue just grinned. In her old school she had also started in the second row, but the conductor had moved her to the first row after a couple of months. She wasn't worried.

Sue was still getting used to high school in the suburbs. Her family used to live in the central area of Seattle, where they had been surrounded by families of various races. Then Sue's father had been promoted, and her mother had convinced him to move to a suburb with bigger and more expensive homes.

"You're an associate professor now," Sue's mother had argued. "We need to entertain a lot more, and we'll need a nicer dining room."

"As long as you cook one of your great Chinese dinners, our guests will be happy," her father had said.

Then her mom had put on a wistful look, the look that never failed. "I've always wanted a big yard with a sunny corner where I can grow roses. I've dreamed about it for years and years."

So Sue's dad had given in. Now their neighbors were mostly white. When Sue started her junior year at Lakeview High, she found the majority of the students to be white. Sue missed her old school, where, if she hadn't exactly been popular, at least she'd been comfortable.

After three weeks at Lakeview, Sue hadn't said much more to her classmates than "Is this seat taken?" The kids weren't mean to her and a few, like Mia, were actually friendly. But even in her old school Sue had been a loner. She didn't make friends as easily as her older sister, Rochelle, who seemed to be able to fit in just by flashing her smile.

When Sue walked from the auditorium to her bus stop, Mia was already standing there. "So did you make it into the orchestra?"

Sue gave a modest smile. "Yeah."

"Great! You'll like Mr. Baxter. Everybody says he's sharp and doesn't miss a single mistake, but he isn't mean when he corrects you."

Suddenly, a deeper voice piped up behind them. "I heard you audition today. Sounded smooth!"

Sue turned around and felt herself blushing. It was the violinist she'd admired—musically *and* physically.

"Thanks," Sue and Mia said at the same time. Sue wondered which of them had impressed him. Or maybe he meant both of them? Maybe he was just trying to be friendly?

The violinist turned to grin at Sue. "Maybe we can set up our instruments and play a duet sometime?"

Sue laughed nervously. He was talking to *her*!

Mia smiled. "Sue, this is Andy Suzuki, our superstar violinist."

Sue opened her mouth, but nothing came out. Luckily, her bus pulled up just then. Looking from the bus to Andy and back, she jumped onto the bus in a daze.

As she slumped into a seat, she replayed his name in her mind. *Andy Suzuki.* There was something about that name. . . . Then, all of a sudden, it hit her with the force of a speeding train. *Suzuki!* He must be *Japanese.* Sue caught her breath, trying to brush it off. *After all, what's wrong with flirting with a Japanese American boy?*

But Sue knew the answer. Her grandmother would *kill* her. And her mother would be furious if she dated a Japanese boy. *That* was what was wrong.

But hey, he was only flirting. He hasn't asked for a date yet. He doesn't even know my last name. Who knows, his parents might be the same way. He might be turned off if he finds out I'm Chinese.

Sue rode home in a daze and spent the rest of the day with her thoughts churning. She answered her parents' questions about school, about the audition, about whatever, but when she went to bed that night, she realized she couldn't remember a word she'd said.

The next morning, when Sue and Rochelle were heading into the school, Mia came up and poked Sue's arm. "You and Andy really seemed to hit it off yesterday."

Rochelle turned to stare at Sue. "Who's Andy?"

Sue shrugged. "Just a violinist in the orchestra."

Mia laughed. "I bet he wants to be more than that," she teased. "I saw the way he looked at you!"

Sue felt her whole body tense. *Shut up, Mia! Not in front of Rochelle!* She spoke between clenched teeth. "Mia, you could have an awesome career writing romance novels! You're so good at creating a big romance out of nothing!"

Mia and Rochelle gaped as Sue stomped off to her homeroom.

For the rest of the morning, Sue was so busy in her classes that Andy faded to the back of her mind. But at lunch, she was standing in line for the hot meal when a deep voice spoke up behind her, making her jump. "I'd better warn you that the chili here is pretty hot. I'd go for the lasagna, unless you like hot stuff."

Andy Suzuki. For a moment Sue's face turned as hot as the chili. "Uh, thanks. I guess I'll take the lasagna."

"Over here!" called Mia from one of the lunch tables after they'd both paid. "We can squeeze in two more."

Sue glanced at Andy and found him smiling back at her. "Shall we?" he asked.

Sue couldn't help smiling back. "Yes, we shall."

As they approached the table, Mia introduced the boy sitting next to her. "This is Nathan. He plays trumpet in the orchestra."

She introduced a couple of other kids at their table, who also played in the orchestra. Soon they were all talking about the trip to Tokyo and whether the school could come up with a way to pay for it.

Sue listened but couldn't bring herself to join in. Even if the school came up with the money, Sue wasn't sure her mother would allow her to go. It would be so depressing to miss out on such a great opportunity. Sue's lasagna seemed to turn to rubber in her mouth.

Andy must have noticed that Sue was preoccupied. "What's the matter, Sue?" he asked quietly. "Something bothering you?"

Sue heard real concern in his voice. *He cares about how I feel.* But Andy was the last person she could talk to about her family problems. "No, I'm fine," she murmured, following it up with what she hoped was a decent imitation of one of Rochelle's smiles.

Later, as Sue and Mia walked to their social studies class, Mia said, "I heard what Andy said at lunch. He's nuts about you."

"Cut it out!" Sue told her. "He was just being nice."

But in the hallway one of Mia's friends had obviously been let in on the Sue-Andy thing.

"Heard you've got a boyfriend, Sue," said Ginny, who played cello in the orchestra.

"He's not my boyfriend!" said Sue, her face growing hot.

"You and Andy are just made for each other," said Mia.

Sue frowned. "What do you mean we're *made* for each other? I just *met* him yesterday!"

Mia looked at Sue. "What's your problem? You're both Asian, aren't you? And you both play in the orchestra. So you're perfect together."

"I'm Chinese!" cried Sue. "Andy is Japanese!"

Suddenly she realized that other kids were turning around to stare. She lowered her voice. "My name is Hua, which is a Chinese name. His name is Suzuki, which is a Japanese name."

"Chinese, Japanese, what's the difference?" asked Ginny.

Sue felt the heat rising in her face. If her mother

heard Ginny talking like this, she'd grab her by the throat and shake her until her teeth rattled.

But then Sue looked around. She realized that everyone was white, except for her and Juan Arroyo, the foreign exchange student. Ginny and Mia couldn't know that much about Asian culture, so they probably weren't aware of the sting their words carried. Sue bit her lip and some of her anger drained away. She'd never really thought about the ways the Chinese and Japanese were different. The two languages were completely different, of course, but that was too complicated to explain. She tried to speak more calmly. "First of all, we wear different clothes. Japanese women wear kimonos, and Chinese women wear cheongsams."

But even as she spoke, Sue realized that clothes were a bad example. Not many Chinese women wore cheongsams these days, and probably even fewer Japanese women wore kimonos. In both countries, the women mostly wore Western clothes.

She tried to think of something else. "The Chinese and the Japanese also eat different kinds of food."

"Aw, come on, you both eat tons of rice, don't you?" said Ginny.

Sue took a deep breath, trying not to get upset. "Even the rice is different. Japanese like short-grained rice that's sticky. We Chinese like rice that's long-grained and not sticky."

"You've got to admit you both use chopsticks," said Mia.

"Our chopsticks are different, too," said Sue. "Ours have flat ends. Japanese chopsticks have pointy ends."

"Come on, chopsticks are just two sticks!" said Ginny. After a moment she added, "Frankly, I can't tell the Chinese and Japanese apart."

Sue lost it then. She felt herself shaking with anger. To somebody like Ginny, with her ash-blond hair and light blue eyes, all Asians probably did look the same.

"That's right!" Sue whispered violently. "All Chinese and Japanese have straight black hair, yellow skin, and slanty eyes! No wonder you can't tell us apart!"

There was an uncomfortable silence. It was a relief when the bell rang and they went to their next classes. Although she was still seething, Sue knew that she had been unfair to Ginny. She herself couldn't always tell whether somebody was Chinese or Japanese or Korean, at least until she learned his or her name. She definitely hadn't guessed that Andy Suzuki was Japanese from just looking at him.

Andy. She thought of the way he'd smiled at her in the lunchroom. His being Japanese didn't make a difference—not to *her.* But it would make a *huge* difference to her mother and to her grandmother.

Sue felt a sudden pang of longing for her old school, where people came in different colors. If she had talked to an Asian boy there, no one would have paid any attention. No one would have decided that the two of them were made for each other.

But what if Andy and I are *made for each other?* Sue closed her eyes and pictured the two of them playing a duet . . . dancing together . . . holding hands at a movie . . .

Stop that! she told herself. She was beginning to think

like Mia and Ginny. All Andy had done was talk to her at the bus stop and sit next to her in the lunchroom. Then she remembered the way he'd looked at her when he'd asked her if something was the matter. He definitely cared.

Sue shook herself. She was thinking way too far ahead. By tomorrow, Andy might be sitting next to somebody else—probably that girl who was his stand partner in the orchestra. They could be . . .

"Going to meet Andy after school?" asked Mia, banging her locker closed.

Sue felt herself thud back to earth. "I wish you guys wouldn't keep talking about me and Andy," she snapped.

"Okay, okay," said Mia. "You don't have to get mad. It'll be our little secret."

"What secret?" asked Rochelle, coming up.

Sue shrugged. "Mia's imagination runs wild sometimes."

Rochelle gave her a look, but to Sue's relief a couple of senior boys came up, and Rochelle abandoned her interrogation.

Sue didn't like keeping things from Rochelle. When they were little kids, Sue and her sister had been close. Rochelle used to read to Sue, and they told each other everything. But things had changed when Rochelle discovered that she was pretty. These days she spent three quarters of her time either looking in the mirror or talking to boys.

* * *

Sue's first rehearsal with the orchestra was Monday after school. She found that the music wasn't all that hard. Mr. Baxter was a good conductor, and Mia was right when she said he was strict but not mean. Even Mia could be fun, when she wasn't winking at Sue and glancing at Andy when he was around.

Andy. As she waited for her bus, Sue had to be honest with herself and admit that he was the main reason she liked the Lakeview orchestra. And she thought about him a lot—the way his eyebrows danced when he was playing a lively passage, the way his eyes almost closed when he was concentrating hard . . .

A deep voice startled Sue out of her reverie. "I'm starving! Want to go to Hero's?"

Sue opened her eyes. Andy stood before her. *He's asking me out!* But before she could get too excited about that, panic struck: *What'll I tell Mom?* Her voice faltered as she said, "It's getting late. My parents might be wondering . . ."

"Aw, come on," he said with a smile, "your folks know you have orchestra after school on Mondays. They don't expect you back too early."

"I *am* pretty hungry," Sue admitted, trying to figure out a way to make this work. *I'm just going to get a sandwich. I don't have to make this into such a big deal!*

" 'S' right," he said. "You need a fuel injection after swinging that viola bow!"

Hero's sandwich shop was just two blocks away, and Sue was relieved when she didn't see Mia, Ginny, or any of the girls who were monitoring the Great Romance. Sue asked for a six-inch, no mustard but plenty of mayo.

Andy ordered a whole hero sandwich with everything on it. He didn't offer to pay for Sue's sandwich. She was kind of relieved, but also a bit disappointed. Did that mean he wasn't asking her out? Was he really only interested in her as a friend?

After Andy took a big bite and wiped the ketchup from his cheek, he asked, "Do you eat mostly Chinese food at home?"

So he *did* know her family was Chinese. He probably knew that Hua was a Chinese name. She wiped her hands and crumpled her sandwich wrappings. "Yeah, my mom cooks Chinese food more than any other kind. How about *your* family? What do you eat, mostly?"

"Let's see. . . . I guess we eat some of everything. My mom likes to try out recipes she sees on TV cooking shows. So we eat Chinese, Japanese, French, Italian—you name it."

Andy didn't seem bothered at all that she was Chinese American, not Japanese American. Sue sighed, thinking about the unfairness of it all. If only things were so simple for *her*!

In the next few weeks, Hero's became a regular Monday-afternoon stop for Sue and Andy. At first, Sue was nervous about what her family would think, but her snacks with Andy remained strictly platonic: a sandwich, a conversation, some warm smiles, and goodbye. Still, Sue was glad that Mia and the others didn't know about Hero's. She was even more glad that Rochelle hadn't found out.

As they ate, they often talked about the pieces they were rehearsing. "I like music with tricky rhythm," said Andy one Monday after they'd rehearsed a Copland piece.

"Me too!" said Sue. "I like certain kinds of jazz, the kind with syncopation. It keeps you guessing, you know?" Andy smiled at her, and Sue's heart did its own syncopation.

Later Sue brought up sports and admitted, "I was always the last one chosen to join a team. I guess people can tell I don't have the killer instinct."

"No team spirit, you mean," said Andy.

"That's true," admitted Sue. "I guess I'm not good at joining the crowd and playing together with others."

Andy grinned. "I hope you play together with the other violists, at least."

Sue laughed. Then she asked, "What do you think about sports? Do you play on any teams?"

"Nope," said Andy. "I avoid sports because I'm afraid of hurting my arm or finger. It would screw up my future as a violinist."

Sue noticed that Andy didn't sound at all embarrassed when he said he was afraid of getting hurt. Most boys would rather die than admit that.

"So you plan to be a professional musician?" she asked.

Andy hesitated. For the first time, Sue saw him looking a little unsure of himself. "I want to, but . . . I've got a problem with stage fright," he confessed. "Every time I have to play a solo, I freak out inside."

"You did great when you were auditioning for that

solo," Sue said, remembering how confident he had seemed.

"I'm okay once I get started," said Andy. "But I'm always afraid that one day I'll be too scared to get started!"

Sue laughed. "It's never going to happen." Without thinking about it, she reached over and put her hand on his arm. Then, suddenly, she felt embarrassed. Andy had never made any kind of romantic gesture toward her. She felt awkward touching him first.

But Andy just smiled and put his hand on top of hers. "What about you? Don't you ever get nervous when you play?"

Sue shook her head. She seldom got really uptight about a recital. Music wasn't her whole life, the way it was with Andy. She had other interests. "I love music, but I love other things, too. You know what fascinates me? The history of warfare. Weird, huh?"

"Hey, my mom is a history teacher!" said Andy. "She teaches at Buchanan Middle School."

They talked about their families. "I have an older brother, Tom," said Andy. "He's a freshman at Oregon State. He's pretty cool. We don't talk much, though, now that he's in school."

"I'm number two in my family, too," said Sue. "My sister, Rochelle, is a senior at Lakeview."

"Guess I'll be running into her," said Andy.

Sue looked down at her sandwich. She wasn't sure how she felt about Andy meeting Rochelle. What if her sister learned that Andy was Japanese and told her mother? Or worse yet, what if Rochelle blinded Andy with one of those killer smiles?

As they were leaving the sandwich shop, Andy stopped at the door. "There's a new anime movie starting in the city on Friday. Want to go? I can pick you up at six o'clock. There'll probably be a long line for the seven o'clock show."

Sue pulled her sweater a little tighter. She so desperately wanted to say yes . . . but how would her mom react when Andy showed up on their doorstep? "Uh . . . uh . . . thanks a lot, Andy, but this weekend is kind of busy. I'm afraid . . ." Her voice trailed off. She couldn't look at him.

He stared at her. "Sure, no problem," he said finally.

He was hurt. Sue wanted to hug him and tell him she was protecting him, not rejecting him. Her mother would say something nasty that would ruin the whole evening. Sue had to figure out how to tell her mother and grandmother about Andy. And she had to do it soon.

2

a ndy shuffled around his living room in a daze. He had been so positive that Sue liked him. So why had she turned him down when he asked her out? He remembered Sue talking to that Ian guy at lunch, making jokes about their math class. Maybe she liked him better. Andy scowled. What was so funny about math, anyway?

Then Andy remembered the shy smile that lifted a corner of Sue's mouth when the two of them talked at Hero's. He thought of the way her eyes sparkled when they talked about a piece of music they both liked. He thought of the way she had put her hand on his, protectively, when he told her about his stage fright. She cared about him. He and Sue had something going, he was sure. But as soon as he'd invited her to go out with him, she'd gotten weird.

Andy decided that after school the next day, he would come right out and ask Sue why she couldn't go out with him.

All the next day, Andy rehearsed the conversation in his head. He wanted to be sensitive, but he also wanted an honest answer. At the bus stop after school, he saw Sue standing with another girl who looked a bit like her but was prettier—and seemed to know it, too. Maybe it was her sister. What did Sue say her name was? Rochelle, that was it. Andy decided to go up and get introduced.

When Sue saw him approach, she looked nervous. Before Andy could speak to her, he heard a voice behind him. "Hey, Andy!" It was Laurie Harris, his stand partner in the orchestra. "I don't see you much after rehearsals anymore. I was hoping to get a little help from you on the Schubert piece. I'm having real trouble with measures fifty-six and fifty-seven, you know?"

Andy felt guilty. He and Laurie were good friends, and they had even gone out a couple of times. They had never gotten really serious, but they'd stayed on good terms. He often went over hard passages in the music with her. A bus came and went as he stood discussing the music with Laurie. By the time he was finished, he turned around and found that Sue had gone.

At dinner that night, Andy was still wondering what Sue's problem was. He was beginning to like her a lot. It wasn't that she was all that incredible to look at. That girl she was talking with at the bus stop—her sister?—was prettier. Sue was a bit skinny, not rounded out like the other girl. But he liked the curtain of shiny black hair falling over Sue's cheeks as she sat with bent head, and her sudden smile when she lifted her head and looked up. Her smile was full of mischief, and he knew that they had the same sense of humor. He liked her soft voice. There was a musical lilt to it. She was a nice change from all the loud girls with their shrieking giggles.

"From your expression, I'm guessing that your practice went well yesterday afternoon," said Andy's mother, interrupting his thoughts. "So you aren't having any trouble with your solos?"

Andy blinked. He realized that he must have been sitting there beaming like an idiot while he thought about Sue. "Solos? Oh yeah, I'm getting through them pretty well, I think. The other soloist is doing okay, too. He's really good!"

"He'd better be good, since he's the concertmaster," said his father. "Frankly, I think you're just as good as he is. But since he's a senior and you're only a junior, the conductor probably feels that you'll get your chance next year."

The best violinist in the orchestra was appointed concertmaster. The concertmaster before this one had been a Chinese American boy, and Andy thought he was a really good musician. After graduating from Lakeview High, the boy had gone on to study at Juilliard, a famous music school in New York.

"Why do so many Asian kids play string instruments?" Andy wondered out loud. "But then our concert-master this year is Caucasian."

"Perhaps more Asians play string instruments because manipulating chopsticks at an early age develops the small muscles of your hand," suggested his father. "That gives you the fine control you need to stop the string accurately on the violin."

"That can't be the reason, Dad," said Andy. "You use chopsticks with your *right* hand, and you stop the strings of the violin with your *left* hand."

"I seem to remember seeing a number of white boys playing the bass fiddle," said his mother.

"You're right," Andy admitted. "Maybe boys think that the bass fiddle is okay because it's so loud and powerful. But they feel like sissies playing the violin."

"Asian kids are not afraid of being called sissies," said his father. "They have more self-confidence."

Andy wasn't sure about that. Some Asian boys, like himself, were resigned to being called nerds anyway, so what did they have to lose by playing the violin?

Andy knew that his father was very proud of his musical talent and had high hopes for him. Andy's grandmother was a good pianist, and whenever they visited his grandparents in California, Andy always begged her to play for him. But his father, to his own disappointment, did not have a gift for music. Neither did Andy's older brother, Tom. Andy was the only one with real musical talent. He did not want to let his father down.

Besides, Andy loved the violin too much to give it up just because somebody might call him a sissy. And he believed that this was true of all music lovers, whether they were black, white, Hispanic, Asian, or Martian.

"Want to go to Hero's again?" Andy asked Sue the next Monday. He tried to sound the same way he always did after rehearsals and pretend that the movie invitation hadn't happened.

Sue hesitated for just a second, then said quickly, "Sure, I'm starved—as usual."

But Andy could see that she was still uncomfortable. After they were seated with their food, he decided he had to find out what the problem was. But first they had to get through the messier part of their sandwiches. When the worst was over for Andy, he wiped the tomato seeds from his chin and cleared his throat. "Can you tell me why you can't go to a movie with me, Sue? Of course, you don't have to say anything if you don't want to."

Sue was silent for a minute. Her head was bent, and her shiny curtain of straight black hair covered her face. Andy could tell, though, that she was very tense. Her fingers clenched her sandwich so hard that some of the innards got squeezed out.

Andy decided to try again. "I like you, Sue, and I want to go out with you. And I think you kind of like me, too. Can you tell me what's wrong?"

Finally Sue raised her head. This time her eyes were not sparkling with their usual smile. "Andy, I can't go out with you because your family is Japanese, and mine is Chinese."

Andy's mouth dropped open. Of all the possible reasons, this was one he had never expected. "Are you kidding? But . . . but . . . we're both Americans!"

"I can't change my heritage, and neither can you, Andy," Sue said softly. "As soon as I entered Lakeview High, the other kids looked at me and said to themselves, 'Hey, we've got a new Asian girl in our class.' "

"And that bothered you?" demanded Andy. "You want to look like Ginny, with blond hair and blue eyes?"

Sue shook her head. "You got me wrong. I'm happy to look totally Asian."

"Then what's the problem?" asked Andy. "We're both Asians, so what's keeping us from going out? If anything, that should make things easier!"

"You're beginning to sound like Mia and Ginny," said Sue with a sigh. "They think we're made for each other, because we both have straight black hair and eat with chopsticks."

Andy had to laugh. "I still don't get it. Okay, so we both use chopsticks. What does that have to do with going out?"

For a moment, the old humorous sparkle had returned to Sue's eyes, but now she became serious again. "I told you already. The problem is that my family's from China, and yours is from Japan. Some of my relatives think that makes us enemies."

Andy stared at Sue, trying to make sense of her answer. He knew that in the 1930s, Japan had invaded China and occupied a large part of the country. And he knew that the occupation had been terrible. But he couldn't believe that something that had happened almost seventy years before could stop him and Sue from going out. The invasion was ancient history!

He took a deep breath. "Look, Sue, some of the musicians in our leading orchestras come from Germany, and some of the other players are Jewish. Their families must talk about how the Nazis in Germany murdered millions of Jews. But this doesn't prevent them from making beautiful music together!"

Sue got up and picked up her viola case. "We can still make beautiful music together, Andy, and eat at Hero's."

Andy gathered his things and followed her to the door. "So, okay, your relatives think of the Japanese as enemies. How about you?"

Sue shook her head. "Of course I don't! You ought to know that by now!"

"I don't get it!" said Andy. "If *you* don't think I'm your enemy, then why are you letting your family keep us from going out?"

"But . . . I . . . I . . ." Sue stopped and took a breath. "It's easy for you to tell me I should stand up to my family. What about *you*? Would you still go out with me if your relatives told you not to?"

Andy blinked. What did his relatives think of the Chinese, anyway? It was a question he had never asked himself.

Just before she reached the bus stop, Sue turned around. "Why don't you ask your relatives how they feel about the Chinese?"

＊ ＊ ＊

Andy decided to do what Sue suggested that very evening. He had never talked to his parents about how they felt about different cultures—not in so many words, anyway. He knew his father had had some bad experiences in different countries as part of his business travels, but he was pretty sure his dad blamed those on individuals, not on whole cultures. "Dad," he said at the dinner table, "you spent a couple of weeks in Beijing last year. What did you think of the Chinese people you met?"

His father was adding some soy sauce to the wasabi for his sashimi. He stopped mixing and looked up. "You've heard me talk about the trip. Beijing was filthy, simply filthy! Except for the big boulevards. The smaller streets were run-down . . ."

Andy's mother broke in. "That's all right, Don, you've told us all we need to know about the filthy streets." She looked at Andy. "Your father didn't have a very good time on the trip. You know that already, so why bring it up?"

Andy's father, who worked for an electronics company, had gone to China on a business trip the previous October. He had come back in a foul mood. The deal he was negotiating had gone through, he said, but the terms were not as good as he had hoped.

Andy remembered that what had made his father even angrier was coming back with his best suit so dirty that he had to pay the dry cleaner extra for getting it back into shape. "My Chinese guide took me on a tour of the Forbidden Palace, and on the way out, we took a back exit and went through a narrow alley," his father said. "The Forbidden Palace is supposed to be the most elegant building in the country. And you know what happened?"

Andy knew what happened. He had heard about the incident many times already. "Right outside the gate," snarled his father, "I tripped on some bricks and fell on a pile of smelly rubbish!"

"I bet the rubbish was organic, at least," murmured Andy's mother.

That didn't help. His father just got angrier. "And the next day, a man in the street hawked and spat on my shoe!"

Andy knew the rest of the story, too. His father was so disgusted that he promptly threw away the shoes and bought a new pair at a Beijing department store. But the new pair didn't fit well, and his feet hurt for the rest of the trip.

"I know all about the spitting and the pile of rubbish," he said impatiently. "What I'm asking is how you feel about the Chinese *people*."

"But that's exactly what I've been saying," said his father. "The Chinese are a dirty people! I bet they don't bathe more than once every other week, if that."

Andy frowned. *A dirty people?* He'd always thought his parents weren't prejudiced, but that didn't sound fair.

Andy's mother laughed. "Remember the story I told you about Queen Elizabeth the First? Some of her subjects thought she was strange because she took a bath once a month, whether she needed it or not!"

Andy tried to laugh, too. "They probably thought

that since she was the queen, she could afford to waste water!"

"As for the rest of the people," continued his mother, "they probably bathed only twice in their lifetime: once as a newborn, and once when they died and their corpse was being laid out."

Andy's father didn't laugh. "Queen Elizabeth lived hundreds of years ago," he said. "I'm saying that the Chinese are a backward people because they don't bathe as often as we do—and I'm talking about today!"

"Don, you have to be fair," said Andy's mother. "We Japanese have a tradition for taking frequent baths because Japan is a volcanic country with many mineral springs spouting hot water. The ancient Romans were big on baths, too, because Italy was volcanic and hot water was plentiful."

"That's the trouble with you historians," grumbled Andy's father. "You like to talk about ancient Romans and Queen Elizabeth the First. I'm talking about the people in Beijing today!"

"Maybe there just isn't enough hot water for the people to take baths every day," said Andy, trying to be fair.

"That proves my point!" said his father. "China is a backward country, just as I said! We Japanese became modernized *years* before the Chinese. We opened our country to the West in the middle of the nineteenth century. We invited Western engineers, scientists, and doctors, and we soon had railroads and electric lights. We built up a modern army and navy that defeated the Russians! What about China at that time? They had those fanatic Boxers who believed they were invulnerable to bullets, and their women still had bound feet!"

Listening to his father, Andy felt depressed. He was disappointed in his dad. At this rate, he didn't think he would be able to introduce Sue to his parents anytime soon.

His mother was different. Her grandparents had moved to America, so she was a third-generation immigrant and thought like an American in most ways.

Andy's father, however, was a Nisei, a second-generation American. Like many other Nisei, he had been sent by his parents to a Japanese high school. Andy thought this was why his father was more Japanese in his opinions—including his attitude toward the Chinese. Andy knew that people in Japan sometimes called the Chinese dirty or backward, but Japan was half a world away. How would Sue feel if she were to hear his own father ranting about how backward the Chinese were?

Andy tried again. He remembered another thing his mother had told him. "The Chinese weren't always backward. Mom says the Japanese didn't have writing until it was introduced from China."

His father was sipping his bean paste soup, but before Andy finished talking, he sputtered and his face grew red. The soup spilled all over the table.

"Get some paper towels, Andy," his mother said.

She didn't have to tell Andy twice. Andy gratefully escaped to the kitchen, and his mother followed him. "Andy, what your father didn't tell you was *why* that man in Beijing spat on his shoe," she said softly. "He only told *me* because I kept asking him why the trip upset him so much. The Chinese man not only spat but also yelled at him. A crowd gathered, and your father's guide had to hustle him away because things were getting ugly. The guide explained afterwards that the man who spat had a brother killed by Japanese soldiers during the occupation. The guide never apologized for the unpleasantness. If anything, he seemed to have enjoyed the scene. Your father was deeply upset by the whole thing."

"It's not Dad's fault that that man's brother was killed," Andy protested. "He wasn't even born yet!"

"*I* know that, Andy," his mother said soothingly. "But the wounds inflicted during a war take a long time to heal. On both sides."

"But that's just one incident!" protested Andy. "Dad shouldn't think *all* the Chinese people are like that!"

"Well, the man who spat on him certainly thought all Japanese people were exactly the same," said his mother. After a moment, she added quietly, "I don't think we should let your father get too angry, Andy. His doctor told us last week that his blood pressure is on the high side, and it's not good for him to get worked up."

Andy wasn't too surprised about his father's high blood pressure. He had seen the tide of red mounting on his father's face. It didn't look healthy. "Okay, Mom," he said. Then he grinned and added, "You know, that's a good way to get the last word all the time. Just tell everybody you have high blood pressure."

"Andy!" said his mother. "You should be ashamed of yourself!" But a moment later, she smiled. "Let's just keep things peaceful at home, all right?"

Andy sighed and made an elaborate bow. "Yes, Mother, this Number Two Son will obey."

His mother smothered a laugh. "You've got the wrong script, Andy. That line comes from an old Charlie Chan movie. It's Chinese, not Japanese."

"So did you find out how your parents feel about the Chinese?" asked Sue the next Monday as she struggled with her salami sandwich.

Andy smiled as he looked at the way Sue licked some mayonnaise from her upper lip. He thought she looked like a cute toddler trying to eat like a grown-up. But his smile faded as he thought back to the way his father had talked about the Chinese. "My mom's okay," he began. "She's a history teacher, like I said, and she knows a lot about how the Japanese learned stuff from the Chinese—things like writing . . ."

"And your father?" asked Sue. "What does he think?"

Andy tried hard to think of a tactful way to express his father's opinions. "My father thinks the Chinese are a backward people," he said finally. He couldn't bring himself to repeat his father's more offensive words about not bathing. Nor did he want to mention the man who had spat and yelled at his father.

Sue took a bite of her sandwich, although she no longer looked hungry. After swallowing she said in a low voice, "I know we're a backward people. During the Second World War, we had very few modern weapons, and that's why your country was able to occupy so much of my country."

Andy was shocked. "Hey, where did this 'your country' and 'my country' stuff come from? I thought we were citizens of the same country! We're both Americans! Or have you forgotten?"

Sue stared at Andy. Then she smiled that little crooked smile he liked so much. "You're right. Whatever happened between China and Japan is history, and we shouldn't let it bother us now."

"Does that mean you'll go out with me?" Andy asked quickly.

Sue's smile disappeared. "Can't we wait just a little longer?"

Remembering his father's anger, Andy had to agree that it might be a good idea to wait. But he hated waiting like this.

As they came out the door of the sandwich shop, they moved aside to make room for a couple who was going in. "Sue!" cried the girl. "What are you doing here? I thought you had orchestra rehearsal!"

Andy recognized the girl as the one he had seen with Sue at the bus stop, the one he suspected was Sue's sister. "Oh, hi, Rochelle," muttered Sue. "We finished rehearsal and got hungry, so we came here for a snack."

Rochelle's eyes narrowed. "*We* got hungry. That doesn't include the rest of the orchestra, obviously. Just you and . . ." She waited.

Andy stepped forward. "Hi, I'm Andy, I'm a violinist. And you are . . ."

"This is my sister, Rochelle," said Sue.

"Fancy not running into you before," drawled Rochelle. "I didn't even know that Sue had a friend."

"I have friends, and you know it!" said Sue. "You even met some of them. Or don't girls count?"

Andy hadn't seen Sue angry before, and he liked her flash of spirit. When her eyes sparkled angrily, she looked beautiful—as beautiful as her sister.

Rochelle raised her hands in surrender. "Okay, okay, you don't have to get mad!" She turned to Andy. "Have you two been coming here a lot?"

Rochelle was obviously fishing for information, and Andy tried to think of a way to head her off without making her too suspicious. "Uh . . . you know how hungry you get after a hard rehearsal . . . ," he began.

Sue jumped in. She turned to the boy with Rochelle and flashed him a big smile. "Fancy not running into you before," she said, in a perfect imitation of Rochelle's drawl. "I didn't even know that Rochelle had a friend."

"Hey, you're pretty good," the boy said to Sue, and laughed. "I'm Jake, by the way."

"Hi, Jake," said Sue, and batted her lashes at him. It was very effective. Sue continued. "You're on the football team, aren't you? You look like an athlete."

"I play soccer," said Jake. "Hey, we have a game—"

"Come on, Jake, let's eat!" said Rochelle, pulling at Jake's arm. "I'm starved!"

After Rochelle and Jake went into Hero's, Andy grinned at Sue. "Your sister sees you as a real threat. She couldn't get Jake away from you fast enough."

Sue gave Andy her usual shy smile, not the flashing one she gave Jake. "First time in my life she saw me as a threat."

"Of course you're a threat!" Andy said as they walked toward the bus stop. "You did a great imitation of Rochelle. You have a good ear."

"I'm sure that'll come in handy someday," said Sue. "You know, I wish I could study some Japanese, now that we might be going to Tokyo. Though I'm still not sure what my mother will have to say about that. Do you speak Japanese at home?"

Andy shook his head. "Not much. My parents tried to teach me and Tom. But Tom complained that he always had too much homework and couldn't take the time, so they gave up." He felt a rush of regret. "I wish they'd kept it up. At least we both learned to read the kana form of writing."

Sue looked excited. "Japanese writing is a lot like Chinese writing, isn't it? I already know some of the characters!"

"The writing that looks like Chinese is kanji, but Japanese also uses a lot of kana, the phonetic writing," said Andy. Seeing Sue's face fall, he added quickly, "I bet you can learn kana in no time. I'll teach you before the orchestra leaves for Tokyo."

Sue's bus arrived, and just before she got on she turned and gave Andy a radiant smile. His stomach twisted—not the sick twist he felt when getting ready to play a solo, but a twist of excitement, like what he felt on the scary Space Mountain ride at Disneyland.

When Sue got home that afternoon, she was surprised to find her mother busily cooking. Usually Sue and Rochelle helped out in the kitchen, starting about an hour before dinner. Sue was the one who washed and cut up the vegetables, while Rochelle did the fine slicing of meat for stir-frying. But from the looks of things today, her mother had been cooking for much of the afternoon.

"Grandma Mei is coming to dinner tonight," she explained.

Sue received the news with mixed feelings. She loved her grandmother deeply. Grandma Mei was chubby and full of bounce. Her face was wrinkled, and since she kept it powdered, she looked like a dried persimmon. Dried persimmons are very sweet, and so was Grandma Mei. But she also had a tart side. And Sue was afraid to hear what the tart side would say if she found out about Andy.

Sue knew that she was Grandma Mei's favorite grandchild. She usually felt overshadowed by Rochelle, who was prettier and made friends more easily. But Grandma Mei always gave Sue an extra warm hug when she visited, and she liked to say that Sue's quiet, modest manner showed that she was growing into a true Chinese lady.

Grandma Mei's visits also meant treats from Chinatown, like dried plums, shrimp chips, or bread stuffed with sweet bean paste. The only thing Sue didn't like about her grandmother's visits was hearing her talk about her painful childhood experiences in China during the Japanese invasion. It always made Sue cringe to picture the horrors her grandmother had suffered. Now, thinking about Andy, Sue dreaded hearing those stories even more.

As soon as Grandma Mei arrived and saw Sue, she smiled until her eyes almost disappeared in her wrinkled face. After giving her a big hug, she asked Sue whether she was keeping up with her Chinese. Sue wanted to please her grandmother, so she said she practiced every Saturday morning. What she didn't mention was that her practice consisted of reading a few Chinese picture books for little kids. But at least she was able to learn some Chinese characters this way.

When Sue's dad came home, he greeted Grandma Mei politely. Sue knew that the two of them didn't have much to say to each other, but they were always polite. Her dad, like most Chinese, treated all old women with great courtesy. And her grandmother, like most Chinese, had great respect for professors. Sue knew that in the old days, only scholars who had passed tough examinations could become officials and run the government. Her father's face still looked young, but his hair had started to turn gray, giving him a look of scholarly wisdom.

"You must be really busy," Grandma Mei said to Sue's father. "So many students to teach!"

"Not so many," said Sue's father. "Thank you for coming all the way across town to visit us."

"Your wife drove me," said Grandma Mei. "So it's no trouble at all."

With this polite exchange out of the way, the family sat down to a Chinese dinner that Sue's mother had started cooking hours earlier. "You didn't have to prepare all these dishes," Grandma Mei told Sue's mother. "After all, I don't eat very much these days."

Sue's mother wiped the perspiration from her face as she put down a dish of chicken and sugar snap peas on the dining table. "I have to show that I haven't forgotten all the cooking lessons you gave me," she told Grandma Mei.

Sue knew perfectly well that this was just another polite exchange. Grandma Mei had to tell her mom that she had gone to too much trouble, but she would have been insulted if an elaborate meal had not been prepared for her.

The dinner was certainly fancier than what the family usually had. That was one of the benefits of having Grandma Mei visit. In addition to the soup, they were going to have five dishes: two cold and three hot. A dish of stir-fried prawns had to be done at the last minute, since it was best when served piping hot.

While Sue's mother was in the kitchen stir-frying the prawns, her father asked for some extra soy sauce. The food was all lightly flavored, since Grandma Mei had to cut down on sodium. Sue went to the kitchen and came back with a small bottle of soy sauce, which she handed to her father.

After splashing a little of the soy sauce on his sliced pork, he put the bottle down on the table. Grandma Mei reached over and read the label. "I don't know this brand," she said. Then she peered harder at the label. "It's a Japanese brand!"

When Sue's mother came in with the steaming dish of stir-fried prawns, Grandma Mei stared at her. "What is this bottle of Japanese soy sauce doing on your dining table?" she hissed. "Did you buy it?"

Sue's mother put down the dish of prawns and hurried over to look at the bottle of Kikkoman soy sauce. "I didn't buy this!"

"*I'm* the one who bought it," said Rochelle. She looked scared. "Remember, Mom? A couple of days ago, you needed soy sauce in a hurry, so I drove down to the Safeway and bought this little bottle. It's a pretty popular brand. Everybody uses it!"

"Come, come, Grandma Mei," said Sue's father. "Kikkoman may have started originally in Japan, but what we get here is actually brewed in . . . let's see . . ." He picked up the bottle and read the fine print. "It's brewed in Wisconsin."

Grandma Mei's face was blotched with patches of red and white. "I don't care where it's brewed! It's a Japanese soy sauce, and I'm shocked to see it on your table!"

Rochelle had turned pale. "I'm s-sorry, Grandma. I was in a hurry and didn't pay any attention."

"I don't think a few drops of Japanese soy sauce will poison us," said Sue's father.

Sue nearly groaned aloud. Her father meant well, but she suspected that his remark would open the floodgates.

She was right. Grandma Mei took a deep breath. "You all take this lightly, because none of you lived through what I did. If you had, you'd hurl this evil bottle out the window!" She reached for the bottle.

Sue's mother quickly took it away. "Now, now, Mother, calm yourself."

"That's easy enough for you to say!" spat Grandma Mei. "You've never been bombed by enemy airplanes, have you? You don't know what it's like to run in fear, while high in the air the pilots giggle and enjoy themselves as they rain bombs on you!"

Sue had been hearing these stories for years and years, but she still hated them. She could picture the panicked Chinese running around on the ground while the Japanese pilots spread death and destruction from above. What she hated most was the thought that Andy shared an ancestry with those bomber pilots. *Maybe if we just sit quietly, Grandma will tire out.*

But Sue's mother had to add her bit. She hated the Japanese almost as much as Grandma Mei because she had grown up constantly hearing these stories. "I agree with you, Mother, that the bombing of civilians is contemptible! It's pure terrorism. Of all the forms of warfare, it is the worst, because its purpose is not to attack the military but to terrorize the people into surrendering."

"The greatest number of civilian casualties was from the atomic bomb at Hiroshima," murmured Sue's father. She was glad he spoke too softly for her grandmother to hear.

"But even worse than the aerial bombing was when soldiers came into our homes," continued Grandma Mei.

Sue knew exactly what was coming next, because her grandmother told this story over and over again. She sighed and got up with Rochelle to clear the table, praying that her grandmother wouldn't cry.

"I still remember the strange quiet," said Grandma Mei. "After weeks of shooting and bombing, our nerves had been shattered by the daily sound of explosions. My parents even made an air raid shelter by digging a trench and covering it with wooden planks. Of course we know now how useless it was, but it gave us a false sense of security. We were lucky that none of the bombs fell near our house. Then one morning, the shooting stopped. It was eerie. We all came out of our houses and looked at one another. At first we thought the Japanese enemy had given up and left, and some of the children started to run around and cheer. Then one of our neighbors told us the truth, that it was the Chinese Nationalist army who had gone. We were left totally defenseless."

Sue and Rochelle sat back down, and Sue's mother set out a platter of cut oranges and cups of tea. Grandma Mei stopped talking to take a sip of tea. When she started again, her voice was less steady. "At first we thought we were safe, and that the Japanese were only interested in going after the army. Then the next day, we heard screaming in the street. We hurried home and bolted the door. It didn't do any good. The Japanese soldiers broke it down and came storming into the house."

"Did they say anything?" asked Sue before she could stop herself. Her grandmother had never mentioned whether the soldiers had tried to communicate. It would have made them seem more human.

Grandma Mei's lips curled. "They had a Chinese interpreter with them, a traitor! They demanded to know whether we had concealed weapons. Then they started searching. Of course we knew they weren't really looking for weapons! They were just looting! My brother and I hid behind the stove in the kitchen, but we could still hear the soldiers throwing things around. When they emptied all our chests and drawers, they made my parents tell them where they had hidden all the money and jewels. My parents told them they had no more valuables, but the soldiers didn't believe them and started to beat them."

Grandma Mei stopped to take another sip of tea. She

swallowed hard, took a deep breath, and continued. "The soldiers finally found nothing valuable left to seize, so they decided to go and loot another house. As they started to leave, I raised my head from my hiding place and peeked out. I saw that one of the soldiers had found my favorite doll. It was only a clay doll, but I loved it because it had such a sweet smile." Her hands began to shake, and some of the tea spilled. "He swung the doll and smashed it against the wall! It shattered into little pieces, and he was laughing like a fiend the whole time!" There were tears running down Grandma Mei's face, and she stopped talking. This was the place where she always stopped.

Sue had often wondered why her grandmother was more upset by the soldier's smashing her doll than by the looting of their valuables and the beating of her parents. Maybe it was because the beating and looting were caused by greed, which was human and which you could at least understand. But smashing the doll was pure cruelty. Truly, a soldier who did that was a beast. And that was what her grandmother thought all Japanese were: beasts.

The family was silent as Grandma Mei wept. Sue squirmed in her seat, wishing there were some way she could help her grandmother. Sue's mother went over to put her arms around Grandma Mei and murmured soothing words. They didn't do any good. They never did.

Suddenly the telephone rang. Rochelle jumped up eagerly. "I'll get it."

Nine times out of ten, the call was for Rochelle, so

nobody else even tried to pick up the phone. Sue could hear her saying, "Yes, this is the Hua residence. . . . You want to speak to *who*?"

Rochelle came back to the dining room looking bemused. "It's for *you,* Sue. Some boy wants to talk to you."

Sue's heart thumped in her chest. *It could only be Andy.* Sue didn't know any other boys well enough for them to call her at home. *But how did he get my phone number?* She could see the surprise on her family's faces as she got up and walked to the hallway. The sadness even faded from Grandma Mei's eyes, and she looked pleased. "A boy? Good for you, Sue!"

Sue's hands were shaking by the time she picked up the phone. For privacy, she retreated into the kitchen and pulled the door shut. "Hello?" she croaked. Then she cleared her throat and said more clearly, "Hello? This is Sue."

"Hi, this is Andy. Is this a good time to call?"

Sue's heart gave another thump. She was thrilled to hear Andy's voice, but she wasn't sure it was such a great idea for him to call her at home—especially on a Grandma Mei night. "Um . . . actually . . . ," she began. "How did you get my phone number, anyway?"

"Uh-oh, caught you at a bad time, huh?" Andy asked. "Well, I know which bus you take. So I looked up all the people called Hua in the phone book who lived in the right neighborhood. Hua isn't that common a name around here."

Sue couldn't believe he'd gone through all that trouble to find her phone number. She heard the murmur of voices in the dining room, and she became nervous. *Can they hear me?*

"Anyway, I called because there's this great jazz concert coming up at Key Arena," said Andy, "and I thought I might try to get tickets for us."

Sue's heart leaped, but she quickly came back down to earth. "I thought we were going to wait a while to go out."

"Yeah, I know," said Andy. "But the concert isn't for a couple of weeks. The tickets are going fast, so I want to get them now."

Suddenly, the kitchen door opened. "Why are you hiding like this?" Rochelle's voice piped up behind Sue.

Sue jumped so hard she nearly dropped the phone. "I'm just talking to a *friend,* do you mind? I thought it would be quieter in the kitchen."

Rochelle was carrying a tray of teacups, and she started loading them into the dishwasher. "Don't let me interrupt you. Go ahead and talk."

"It's too noisy in here," Sue said into the phone. "Let's talk tomorrow. There's something I have to tell you."

"Okay, I get the idea," said Andy. "We'll talk at lunch, all right?"

"All right," breathed Sue. She hung up, turned around, and found Rochelle staring at her.

"Kind of jumpy, aren't you?" Rochelle asked. "What is it that you don't want us to hear?"

Sue tried to control her temper. "*You* may enjoy talking to everyone about your boyfriends, but I don't."

Rochelle grinned. "Then the guy on the other end of the line *is* your boyfriend! Why do you have to keep him secret?"

When Sue hesitated, Rochelle's face became serious. "Sue, is something wrong? You've been kind of weird lately. Are you in some kind of trouble?"

Rochelle's face looked so solemn, Sue had to suppress the urge to laugh. Before she could say anything, Rochelle came over and put her arms around her. "Sue, you're not, like, into drugs or anything? I won't tell Dad or Mom if you don't want me to, but you can come to me with anything, you know."

This time, Sue had to concentrate on not cracking up. She knew Rochelle meant well, but she was so far off the mark it was ridiculous. She knew kids at school who smoked pot or took ecstasy, but using drugs wasn't something that had ever interested her. She never felt like doing something just because others did it.

"Or is it something to do with the boyfriend himself?" asked Rochelle gently. She paused, and then whispered, "Is he . . . you know . . . putting pressure on you to . . . you know . . ."

This time, Sue couldn't hold back her giggles. She put her hand over her mouth to smother her laughter.

Rochelle dropped her arms and stood back. "Well, excuse me for asking! I didn't know it's all a big joke!"

Sue saw the hurt on Rochelle's face and felt bad. She realized how far apart she and Rochelle had grown. She remembered how she used to run to her sister and tell her everything. She'd always been able to count on her to listen sympathetically. "Rochelle, wait!"

Rochelle turned around and looked at Sue. "What is it, Sue?" she asked quietly.

Sue took a deep breath. "You're right, the problem is with Andy."

"Andy? The boy I saw you with at Hero's?"

Sue nodded. "His name is Andy Suzuki, and he's Japanese American."

Rochelle was quiet for a minute, and then whistled. "I get it. You think Mom would freak out if she knew."

Sue nodded again. After a long silence, Rochelle spoke. "Look, Sue, you and Andy aren't exactly running off to get married tomorrow. I mean, he's just asking you for a date." She peered at Sue. "Right?"

"I don't want Mom to know I'm seeing a Japanese American boy," Sue said miserably. "Please don't tell her, Rochelle."

Rochelle sighed. "Okay, I won't tell her. But you can't keep this a secret forever. She'll want to know who you're going out with. She asks about my boyfriends all the time."

Sue smiled. "No, she doesn't. She's given up trying to keep track."

Rochelle smiled back, then turned serious. "Look, Sue, take my advice and come clean soon. Maybe not tonight when Grandma's around, but soon. It's easier on the nerves—especially *my* nerves. Besides, I don't think Mom can hate the Japanese forever. Dad can talk her around."

"Mom's been brainwashed about the Japanese from the day she was born!" said Sue. "No matter how I tell her, she's going to freak out. And if she knew about Andy, she'd tell Grandma."

"So she'll tell Grandma," said Rochelle, and shrugged. "It's not the end of the world. So she'll be a little upset."

Sue thought of the incandescent hatred on Grandma Mei's face, so intense that you could almost feel it radiating across the room. If Grandma knew Sue was dating a Japanese boy, she would be devastated. "I can't hurt Grandma like that, Rochelle."

Rochelle looked exasperated. "I don't get why you care so much about what Grandma Mei thinks! It's *your* life! And it's not like she's *living* with us!"

Sue shook her head. *Rochelle doesn't care about Grandma. She isn't close to Grandma, like me.* "Please, Rochelle," said Sue. "For me, just keep quiet about Andy!"

Rochelle sighed. "All right, Sue. I won't be the one to blow the whistle."

Come clean soon. Later that night, as Sue unloaded the dishwasher, she kept thinking about Rochelle's words. She knew she had to tell her mom about Andy sooner or later. But when?

After driving Grandma Mei home, her mother came into the kitchen and began to put away the leftovers. "So that was your boyfriend you were talking to?" she said brightly to Sue. "What's his name?"

"Uh ... uh ... Andy," said Sue. "His name's Andy, and he plays first violin in the orchestra."

"Good, good," said her mother.

Before her mother could ask more, Sue took a deep breath. "Mom, are you really upset about our orchestra planning a trip to Tokyo?"

Her mother put down the dish of leftover prawns.

There was a silence. "You know how I feel about the Japanese, Sue," she said finally. "I hate the very thought that you'd be breathing the same air as those people."

"But Mom," protested Sue, "the people in Tokyo today aren't the same ones who invaded China!"

Her mother's face was stony. "I know how much the orchestra means to you, so I'm not stopping you from making the trip—if it's really in the works. But I don't want to talk about it anymore!"

This was definitely not the right time to tell her mother about Andy's last name.

At lunch the next day, Sue and Andy sat alone at their own table, away from Mia, Ginny, and the others. They both knew they had to talk. Andy started speaking before he even unwrapped his sandwich. "I'm beginning to like you a lot, Sue. If my dad had a bad time during his trip to China, he can get over it! I know that our families have their own weird prejudices. But we can't let them control us. If you come over and meet him, he'll see that not all Chinese are the same."

"The same as what?" asked Sue.

Andy looked down and pulled at a piece of lettuce in his sandwich. "My dad said somebody spat at him," he muttered, finally.

Sue felt herself growing angry. "So. We're backward, and we spit in the streets. That's just great."

"Hey, what's up with this 'we' stuff?" protested Andy. "One Chinese guy spat on my father once. That doesn't mean anything about you, or about your family. Besides, I thought we'd agreed that we were *Americans* before anything else."

Sue tried to take a bite of her sandwich but put it down again. "We are, but that doesn't mean we can shake off our cultural heritage."

Andy snorted. "Heritage, shmeritage! You're beginning to sound like a social studies teacher!"

Seeing that Andy was growing more and more impatient, Sue tried to explain. "It's not just the heritage thing. My mom really hates the Japanese. See, my grandmother was in China during the Japanese invasion. It was a terrible experience, and it really scarred her. She tells us about it every chance she gets. You can imagine what it's like for my mom, who's been hearing all that since she was a baby."

Andy frowned and nodded sympathetically. He didn't seem to know what to say. Sue drank some of her milk. She was so miserable that she didn't see how she could finish her sandwich.

Finally Andy said quietly, "Tell me about what happened to your grandmother. I've read *The Rape of Nanking*. Was she . . ." He stopped, then started again. "Was she . . . um . . . raped by the invaders?"

Sue shook her head. She knew that abuse of Chinese women had been common during the Japanese invasion, but Grandma Mei's family had been lucky, at least in that respect. She told him about the bombings and the soldiers breaking in and the beating. Andy looked a little pale when Sue finished. "How badly were they beaten, your . . . let's see . . . your great-grandparents?"

Sue's grandmother had gone into a lot of detail during some of her visits. "Badly. Her father's arm was broken, and her mother lost a couple of teeth. I can imagine how horrible it must have been for her to watch and not be able to do anything." After a moment, she added, "But the thing that always makes my grandmother cry is when she talks about how one of the soldiers smashed her favorite doll. It just represents the whole terrible experience for her. What kind of monster would destroy some little kid's favorite toy?"

This time the silence between them lasted even longer. Andy was first to speak. "I know that terrible things went on during the Japanese invasion. Do you think I might be a monster like those soldiers?"

Sue quickly shook her head. "I don't believe that *you* could ever be like that," she protested.

"But do you think my *family* could be like that?" continued Andy.

Sue took a breath and tried to think. What *did* she believe? She tried to picture the men who had beaten her great-grandparents. Had they been anything like Andy? Could that kind of cruelty really be carried in the blood?

She'd grown up listening to her grandmother's stories, never quite believing that all Japanese were evil but still unable to explain the cruel acts of the Japanese soldiers. She knew Andy would never behave that way, but the truth was that she *wasn't* sure what she felt about the Japanese people.

She looked into Andy's eyes, and for the first time she saw not understanding but anger. She realized with a sickening thud that her hesitation was really hurting him. How did it feel when a person you liked thought you came from a race of monsters? Sue wanted to open her mouth and explain, but she was afraid that it was already too late.

Andy took a deep breath. "Let me tell you a little about my family. My mother's grandparents came over from Japan, and they became truck farmers. During the Second World War, her grandfather and his whole family were rounded up as enemy aliens and put in a camp."

Sue couldn't seem to push any words out of her mouth. She had heard about the so-called relocation camps, called concentration camps by some people. The Japanese immigrants on the West Coast were imprisoned there under harsh conditions because there was doubt about their loyalty to their new country.

Andy continued, his voice low but shaking with anger. "My grandfather was able to leave the camp when he enlisted in the army—the *American* army. He fought in Italy, where he was wounded. The American government awarded him the Purple Heart. Does he sound like the kind of monster who terrorized your grandmother?"

Before Sue could think of anything to say, Andy stood up abruptly and left the lunchroom.

The next orchestra rehearsal was almost a week away, so it would be several days before Sue and Andy could have a private talk at Hero's. Sue decided to approach him during lunch the next day to apologize. She felt terrible for making him so angry.

At lunch, though, Andy sat at a different table. He didn't even glance in Sue's direction as he walked by with his tray. Mia's eyebrows rose so high they practically disappeared into her hairline. "Hey, why is Andy sitting over there?" she hissed to Sue.

"Maybe he got tired of your jokes about being my boyfriend," snapped Sue. She knew she was being unfair, but she couldn't bear to tell Mia and Ginny about the fight with Andy. How could either of them understand?

At lunch the next day, Sue saw Andy come into the cafeteria. This time she turned her head away and pretended to ignore him. She was angry now; she had wanted to apologize, but that was before Andy had started acting like such a jerk. She didn't want him to know that she was watching for him. She hoped that maybe Andy would stop to talk—how long could he stay mad?—but it didn't happen. If anything, he brushed by her table even faster than the day before.

And so it went on like that. Sue felt worse with Friday's lunchtime snub. She even considered marching up to Andy and confronting him. But then she remembered the anger on his face when he had stormed away from her. She didn't want to fight with Andy in front of everybody. It would just have to wait until Monday.

"All right, Sue, what's going on with you and Andy?" Mia asked at lunch when Andy again sat down at another table.

"What do you mean?" mumbled Sue, although she knew perfectly well what Mia meant. It was obvious to anybody with eyes in their head that almost overnight Andy had gone from being crazy about her to hating her. Suddenly, she felt hot tears well up in her eyes. "Got to go to the bathroom," she blurted, and bolted to the girls' room before the tears could spill down her cheeks.

As she stood wiping her eyes with a paper towel, Mia came in. "You and Andy had a fight, didn't you?" she asked gently. "You can't stay mad at each other like this, Sue. You've got to do something."

"Because we're just made for each other?" snapped Sue. "Because we're both Asian Americans?"

Mia came over and put her arms around Sue. "Listen, Sue, now that I really know you and Andy, I don't think of you as Asian American, or whatever. You're just *you*. What I *do* know is that Andy likes you a lot. I can tell he's really upset about the fight you had. Whatever he did to make you mad, get over it!"

Sue shook her head. "That's just it. It isn't something Andy did. The problem is with our folks. Andy's family is from Japan, and mine is from China. They think that makes us enemies."

Mia stared. Her mouth opened and closed, so that she looked like a goldfish. "Are you serious? You're telling me that you broke up with Andy just because your family didn't approve of him?"

When Mia put it like that, Sue had to admit that it seemed stupid—especially since her family hadn't even *met* Andy yet.

"You know what this reminds me of?" said Mia. "*Romeo and Juliet.* How the two lovers have to meet in secret because their families are feuding. Are you making yourself out to be Juliet?"

Sue's tears had dried, and she found herself smiling. "Okay, Mia. I get it. Just promise you won't start calling Andy Romeo."

as soon as the orchestra members were seated at Monday's rehearsal, Mr. Baxter gave them a big smile. "Well, folks, I just got word that your parents will be meeting next Tuesday to discuss the trip to Japan. If they manage to work something out, we've got Tokyo in our sights!"

The players cheered, and the rehearsal started with a bang. Mr. Baxter launched the orchestra into the noisiest piece they knew. He drove his players so hard that they were practically panting at the end of the piece. But nobody complained. They all shared the excitement of knowing that the trip might really happen.

In the viola section, Sue was too busy thinking about

her fight with Andy to play her best. When the rehearsal ended, Sue started walking automatically over to Hero's. Andy usually caught up with her before she was halfway there, and even though she knew he was still mad at her, she was hoping against hope that he would show up anyway. If he followed her to Hero's, they would have privacy, and Sue could finally apologize. She could tell him that whatever her mother or her grandmother thought about the Japanese, she liked and trusted him, and that was all that mattered.

The last of the orchestra members were leaving the school. Sue walked slowly toward Hero's, looking back every now and then to check for Andy. She was almost at the sandwich shop and there was still no sign of him.

Finally she saw him. She felt her heart quicken as she saw him pulling on his jacket as he walked out of the school. But then Sue realized that not only was he not following her to Hero's, but he was not alone. He and a girl were busy talking, apparently discussing some musical passage. Sue recognized the girl as Laurie, his stand partner. Andy made bowing motions with his arm, and Laurie did the same. Then Andy nodded at Laurie, she said something, and they both burst out laughing.

Sue felt her face grow hot. Laura might be Caucasian, but it seemed that she had a lot more in common with Andy than Sue did.

How could I be so stupid! She had been so angry when Mia and Ginny and the others assumed that she and Andy were made for each other because they were both Asian. But watching Andy laugh at Laurie's jokes, Sue realized that she herself had assumed the same thing! And she had been just as wrong as Mia and Ginny.

But wait a minute. Sue remembered the concern in Andy's voice when he'd asked her in the lunchroom whether anything was the matter. He really did care about her. Or did he? Sue was so torn that she didn't know what to believe. The only thing she knew for sure was that she was alone, and she was totally miserable.

She couldn't face entering Hero's and having Andy snub her yet again. She hurried over to the bus stop, her eyes filling with angry tears.

Andy waved and called to Sue, but she kept walking and didn't look around. He stopped trying to attract her attention when he saw her step up into the bus. Her head was bent, and she looked so forlorn that he felt a pang of guilt.

"So you think those short, choppy notes aren't going to work?" said Laurie's voice beside him.

Andy pulled himself together. "Short, choppy . . . ? Oh yeah, right. That's the way we should do it."

Laurie grinned. "Can't concentrate? Okay, I'll let you go. I've got to run anyway."

After Laurie left, Andy realized that even though Sue had gone, he was still really hungry. He walked slowly to Hero's. It felt funny to go in and eat by himself. Apparently the boy making sandwiches thought so, too. "What happened to your girlfriend?" he asked. "Had a fight, huh?"

"Mind your own business," growled Andy. Ignoring the boy's smirk, he took his sandwich and walked over to his and Sue's usual table.

He knew their fight hadn't been Sue's fault, not totally. He couldn't blame her for being upset, since he'd started sitting at a different table during lunch. He had been really angry with her after their argument. Sue had said it was only their families keeping them apart, but the more she said it, the more it sounded as though *she* had some problems with the Japanese people, too.

But then he thought about it. He realized he wasn't being really fair to Sue. If that man in Beijing, instead of just spitting on Andy's father, had also broken his arm and knocked out some teeth, Andy would have to think for a moment on how he felt about the Chinese people.

Sue was right about one thing, anyway: it was too soon for her to introduce him to her family. He would have to find a chance to talk to her. He was reluctant to approach Sue in school, where Mia, Ginny, Nathan, and others had their sharp eyes on them. He'd have to continue meeting her at Hero's after rehearsals—if he could get her to join him again.

Tuesday night was the night of the meeting to discuss how to finance the trip to Tokyo. Andy and his parents showed up at the school gym right on the dot at seven-thirty, but the tiers of seats were already crowded, and they had to go all the way to the top row to find room. Andy looked around to see if he could find Sue. Since he was looking down on the backs of people, he wasn't able to spot her.

The meeting was chaired by a Mrs. Fulton, the president of the Lakeview P.T.A. "Ladies and gentlemen," she said, calling the meeting to order, "you all know why we are here. As you no doubt recall, the Kasei School from Tokyo visited America last year and gave a concert at our school. Most of the people here went to that concert, which was a huge success. The Kasei School is noted for its outstanding musical program. Its orchestra played superbly, and deserved the enthusiastic reception they got." She paused, looked around, and smiled. "I believe that the Lakeview High School Orchestra is every bit as good!"

Wild applause broke out. Personally, Andy thought that the Kasei orchestra had a stronger wind section, but the Lakeview orchestra had better string players.

The year before, his parents had acted as host family for a cellist from the Kasei orchestra. Since their guest spoke very little English, Andy's father had to do most of the talking. On the weekend the Suzukis took their guest for a picnic on Mount Rainier, and the snowy scenery impressed him deeply. He kept saying, "Fuji! Just like Mount Fuji!"

Andy wondered if he would see the boy again if he went to Tokyo. Then he remembered that the boy had been a senior and would have graduated by now. Did Sue's family also host a player from the Kasei orchestra? No, of course not. Sue had just transferred to Lakeview High and hadn't been around during the visit by the Japanese kids.

Meanwhile, Mrs. Fulton was still talking. "As you know, our orchestra has received an invitation from the principal of the Kasei High School to visit Tokyo and give a concert in their auditorium."

More applause. Without waiting for it to end, Mrs. Fulton went on. "We are on the point of accepting the invitation, but before we can do so, there is the problem of financing the trip. We don't have to worry about lodging, since host families in Tokyo have offered to put up our players. But we still have to pay for the plane tickets."

"How did the Kasei orchestra pay for their trip?" asked one of the parents.

"A good question," said Mrs. Fulton. "I actually asked the Kasei principal. He said that the parents of the players paid for all the tickets."

There was a murmur from the audience. Andy turned and looked at his father. "Of course I'll pay for your ticket!" his father said. "It doesn't cost any more than the music camp you've been attending for the last three years!"

"Mrs. Fulton, we should not forget that Kasei is a private school, where wealthy parents send their kids," said a parent. "Let's remember that Lakeview High is a public school, open to students of all backgrounds!"

"Not everybody here can afford a round-trip plane ticket to Tokyo at the drop of a hat," said another voice.

"There is something else," said Mrs. Fulton. "Japanese parents typically spend a lot more money on their children than we do, I am told. Many families have only one child, or at most two, so they tend to spend more on each child."

"We have families here with three, four, or more children," said another parent. "We can't all afford to buy tickets to Tokyo. I don't think it would be fair if only players from rich families go to Japan."

"I think I can safely say that we all agree with you," said Mrs. Fulton. "Therefore, we are here tonight to think of some way to find money for the tickets for *all* the players."

"Hear, hear!" came from a number of parents.

"All right, we're agreed on that," said Mrs. Fulton. "One way of raising money is to go door to door and solicit."

"By ringing every doorbell in the school district, we'll involve the whole community in the orchestra's visit to Japan," said another parent. "I think this is a good idea."

"If you just ring doorbells and ask for money, people might give you one or two dollars," objected a parent. "We'd have to get contributions from *thousands* of people to pay for all the tickets!"

Andy groaned. He pictured himself ringing doorbells and saying with a bright, toothy smile, "Hi, how would you like to contribute some money to help send the Lakeview High School Orchestra to Japan?"

Other suggestions were made: a bake sale, a car wash. It was decided that none of these schemes would produce enough money in time for the trip.

"How about an auction?" suggested one parent. "If you just ask for money, people will give you only one or two dollars. But they'll offer a lot more money if you can give them something they want."

"Hey, that's not a bad idea!" said several people. Mrs. Fulton made the motion to adopt the proposal and was seconded. "Shall we have a show of hands?" she asked. The motion was approved by such a large majority that it was unnecessary to count the votes. It was decided that there would be an auction, and that the orchestra members would also solicit donations door to door and hold a car wash to increase their chances of raising enough money.

After the meeting ended, Andy and his parents got up from their hard wooden bench and went down to the floor of the gym. They joined the other parents and stood around talking, mostly about what they could contribute for the auction.

"I can offer a gourmet dinner for six," offered one mother.

"Yeah? And who's going to do the cooking?" asked her husband.

One couple said they would offer tickets to some Seattle Seahawks games, while another couple offered a week at their beach cabin.

Andy had a sudden vision of bidding for the beach cabin and staying there with Sue. They could swim all day, barbecue some burgers for supper . . . and then the picture became . . . well . . . exciting. He realized that he was breathing fast and tried to focus on what the other parents were saying.

He moved toward the refreshment table to get some juice—some ice-cold juice. Was he still daydreaming, or was it really Sue at the other end of the table?

She was standing with a middle-aged couple, and from the family resemblance, Andy guessed that they were Sue's parents. Andy eagerly studied the woman, Sue's mother, realizing that she was his potential enemy. She had a smile similar to Sue's. She was petite and looked calm and pleasant—not at all the kind of person who might attack him for being Japanese. He wondered whether Sue had been exaggerating about her mother. Should he try to attract Sue's attention and get introduced to her parents?

"I feel that the auction should also include some valuable objects, not just services," said Andy's father, approaching the refreshment table and pouring himself a cup of coffee.

"Maybe someone has a piece of art he wants to offer," said one of the mothers. "I mean, something other than what you'd find at garage sales."

"I have a hand-embroidered blouse I can contribute," said one woman.

"I do ink brush paintings," said a woman behind Andy. "I can offer one of my works, if someone thinks it's worth it."

Andy turned around and saw that the speaker was Sue's mother. Standing next to her was Sue. She looked up, and her eyes met Andy's.

Should he say something to her? They hadn't spoken for more than a week, and Andy still remembered his anger as he stormed out of the lunchroom at school. He also remembered the sadness in Sue's face when he saw her after rehearsal the day before. What was she thinking now?

There was no doubt about it: from her panicked expression, Sue didn't think it was time for her parents to meet Andy and his family. She looked ready to make a run for it.

"You do ink brush paintings?" Andy heard his father say. He saw that his father had stepped over to Sue's mother and was addressing her. "That's wonderful! These days there are too few artists using this medium. Most of them go in for oil paintings."

Sue's mother looked pleased. "I'll never turn to oils. I do only black-and-white ink brush painting."

Andy's father nodded. "Black-and-white brush painting is what I like best, too! The brushwork has a flexibility and strength that you also see in calligraphy. I would love to bid on one of your works!"

Andy groaned inwardly. He could see what was coming next. His father would ask the artist's name. He had simply assumed, of course, that a woman cultured enough to do ink brush painting was Japanese. While Sue's mother probably assumed that only a Chinese man would have the sensitivity to appreciate this kind of painting.

But once they got introduced, the two would realize that their respective names were Hua and Suzuki. What then?

Again, Andy looked at Sue, to see how she felt. She shook her head very slightly. Apparently she had seen the dangers, too, and didn't want to take a chance.

"Mom, I've got a headache coming on," Sue said. "Can we go home?"

"Oh, all right," said Sue's mother, reluctantly tearing

herself away from someone with such good taste. She turned to a gray-haired man, who had to be Sue's father. "Shall we go?"

Andy didn't know whether he was relieved or disappointed. A potential scene had been avoided, but he had also lost the opportunity to talk to Sue and end their fight. He couldn't wait until the next rehearsal. He would have to think of some other way to approach her.

The door-to-door campaign began after school two days later. As Sue started her route, she wondered if Andy's was anywhere near hers. He had told her which bus he took, and she knew he didn't live too far off. What would she do if she ran into him? At the meeting in the gym, he had looked like he wanted to talk to her, and maybe make up. Or was she just imagining things? She sighed and took out her forms. *I've got to stop obsessing about this and get down to work.*

Going door to door turned out to be not as bad as she expected. She tried her own neighborhood first, people she knew. First she tried the house at the end of her block, the Dawson family. She took a deep breath and rang the bell. The daughter, who was a ninth grader at Lakeview, opened the door. "Hi, Judy," said Sue. "I'm raising money for—"

"I know!" said Judy with a big grin. "The orchestra is going to Japan." She turned around and called out, "Mom, it's someone raising money for the orchestra's visit to Japan!"

Mrs. Dawson came to the door. "Hello . . . it's Suzanne Hua, isn't it? So the Lakeview orchestra has been invited to play in Tokyo. What a great honor! And for you, going to Japan must be almost like going home!"

Mrs. Dawson meant well, so Sue didn't have the heart to say that Japan was totally different from China, and that going there was not at all like going home. America was her home.

Mrs. Dawson contributed five dollars, not a bad start. After that, Sue lost much of her nervousness. At a couple of houses nobody was home. When she reached the house owned by a crabby old man who was always shooing cats away from his yard, Sue hoped that he would be out. But he was home. When he opened the door, Sue didn't have a chance to start her spiel before he snapped, "Whatever it is, I don't want any!" and slammed the door in her face. But at most houses, Sue's reception was pretty friendly, even when she didn't manage to get a contribution.

Around suppertime, Sue decided to call it quits. People hated having their meals interrupted, and besides, she was so tired she couldn't face climbing any more front steps. Playing her viola for the same number of hours didn't tire her half as much. She had covered only a small part of her route, the part closest to home. She looked at her total: not quite forty dollars. She didn't know how much one round-trip ticket to Tokyo cost, but with forty kids in the orchestra . . . Well, they could still make money from the car wash and the auction.

At supper, Sue was almost too tired to eat. But after a few bites of her mother's soy chicken, she recovered some of her energy. "So how much money did you get?" asked Rochelle.

"About forty dollars," mumbled Sue.

"Hah!" said Sue's mother. "At this rate, you won't make enough money even for half a ticket, much less to pay for the whole orchestra to go."

"We still have other ways of raising money," Sue pointed out. "I'm going to do some car washing next week, and there's still the auction."

"I still think the whole scheme is hopeless!" said her mother.

Sue knew that her mother hated the idea of the trip and would be delighted if the orchestra failed to get enough money. But at least she had agreed to allow Sue to go.

Sue and Rochelle were just clearing the table when the doorbell rang. "Maybe it's one of our orchestra members asking for money," muttered Sue, going to the front door. "I'll have to tell him that this is one house that's already made its contributions!"

When Sue opened the door, she was stunned to see Andy standing there. For a minute, the two of them just stared at each other. Finally Andy broke the silence. "I guess this is one house that's already made its contributions, huh?"

On hearing her own words, Sue broke into giggles that had a touch of hysteria.

Andy looked nonplussed. "I came here tonight because I wanted a chance to talk to you, Sue," he said finally.

Sue had waited so long to speak to Andy, but now that they were face to face, she found her throat getting tight. She tried for a light tone. "We had a close call at the gym. I thought your dad and my mom were going to figure out what was going on with us, and then we'd have a duel with drawn swords."

Andy grinned. "Yeah, maybe I could get my dad to use a samurai sword! That'd be the most spectacular event the Lakeview gym ever had!" His face became serious. "Sue, I came here to tell you how sorry I am about what's happened between us. It was dumb of me not to sit with you at lunch. At first, I was just so mad, and then once I realized what a jerk I was being, I guess I was too proud to apologize. I meant to talk to you after rehearsal the other day, but I had to stop and go over something with Laurie. You were gone before I had a chance to say anything to you."

So Andy isn't interested in Laurie after all. She's just his stand partner, and needed his help with some music. The rock that had been lodged in Sue's chest since their last rehearsal seemed to dissolve. "I haven't been all that nice to you, either. What I said to you about the Japanese soldiers was pretty unfair to your family."

"I thought it was *your* turn to scrub the pots, Sue," said Rochelle, coming to the door. "What's taking you so long? Can't you just tell him this house has already made its contributions?"

Both Andy and Sue broke out laughing. Rochelle

stared at them. "Hey, you're Andy, right? You called Sue the other night, didn't you?"

Rochelle was studying Andy, and Sue knew that she was sizing him up.

"Yeah, we met after one of our rehearsals," Andy replied. "I play first violin in the orchestra."

"Sue told me your last name is Suzuki," said Rochelle.

There was a pause. Andy glanced at Sue, a question in his eyes. "No, I haven't told my mother yet," muttered Sue.

Andy backed down the steps. "Well, I better go try a few more houses before packing it in for the night." He waved at Rochelle and smiled. "Nice seeing you again."

"He seems okay, your Andy," remarked Rochelle. "I think you should have asked him in to meet Mom and Dad."

"Maybe I'd better go ring a few more doorbells, too," said Sue, hurriedly changing the subject.

But before she could leave the house, she was way-laid by her mother. "Didn't I hear somebody at the door?"

Rochelle answered first. "It's Sue's boyfriend. He came over especially to talk to her."

Her mother smiled. "Your boyfriend, Sue? Is this the boy who called the other night? Your father and I would have enjoyed meeting him. Why didn't you bring him in and introduce him?"

"That's exactly what I want to know," said Rochelle. "Why didn't you bring Andy in and introduce him?"

"Andy, is that his name?" said her mother. She

seemed eager to know more. Sue had gone out with a few boys in her old school, but she had never had anyone she could really call a boyfriend. This was the first time a boy had come to see Sue after they moved to the new neighborhood.

"He was in a hurry to ring more doorbells," explained Sue, before her mother could ask for Andy's last name. "I'm in a hurry, too."

She grabbed her name tag and forms and dashed out the door.

But she knew she couldn't play these delaying games for long. Sooner or later, her parents were going to learn that her boyfriend was Japanese American.

for weeks Andy knocked himself out ringing doorbells
and washing cars. He had hardly any time left for practicing. During one rehearsal, he missed some notes in his
solo, something he had never done before.

Raising money for the orchestra made him realize
something. One day, as he was rinsing the soap from a
car, the owner smiled at him and said, "So you're going
to Japan! It must be like looking for your roots, huh?"

Until that moment, Andy had simply thought of himself as an American, and didn't spend much time wondering about his roots. His father often tried to tell Andy
about his Japanese ancestry, but Andy got the feeling he
didn't act as interested as his dad would have liked.

Andy's paternal grandfather had been born in Japan. He was able to get a scholarship to attend a college in the States under a program sponsored by the American occupation after the war. In Seattle, he'd met Andy's grandmother, a Japanese American girl majoring in music and studying the piano.

Andy's grandmother loved to tell the story of how she and his grandfather had fallen in love. At a party, she had noticed a lonesome young Japanese boy whose English wasn't good enough for him to mingle. She felt sorry for him, so she went over to the piano and played some Japanese folk songs to cheer him up. This touched him so deeply that he almost broke down and cried. She in turn was so touched by his reaction, she almost cried herself. The rest, she liked to tell Andy, was history.

Andy's grandfather stayed in America after getting married, but he never got over his homesickness for Japan. He would tell his children Japanese fairy tales, while Andy's grandmother played Japanese songs. Andy's father grew up speaking Japanese at home. His grandfather would point out to his grandchildren how, every year on December 7, Americans remembered Japan's preemptive strike at Pearl Harbor. However long the Suzukis had been in America, Andy's grandfather insisted, they were still regarded by some people as enemy aliens.

Listening to his grandfather talk like this, Andy wasn't surprised that people in America thought of him as an alien. Andy thought of Pearl Harbor as just another incident in American history, not something that had much to do with him personally. Occasionally he felt that people made assumptions about him because he was Asian, but he never felt that anyone discriminated against him because his ancestors were Japanese.

The story of Andy's mother's family was very different from his father's. During World War II, her family, like many West Coast Japanese Americans, had been forced into "relocation" camps. The American government felt that Japanese Americans were too Japanese to be trusted. The camps were situated in bleak, remote parts of the country, and living conditions were harsh. In spite of this, her grandfather still thought of himself as a patriotic American, and had even fought in the U.S. Army.

At home, Andy tended to side with his mother. She was easier to get along with in general. He remembered her saying, "If you're really looking for slights or insults, you can always find some. But why bother?"

Andy's mother was a history teacher, so she took a wider and longer view of things. Whenever Andy's father started growling about discrimination by white people, she was always able to point out even worse cases of discrimination at some other place in some other time.

The doorbell ringing and car washing made Andy start thinking about the trip as an opportunity to see the country of his ancestors. Of course, his father had made sure that he and his elder brother weren't totally ignorant of Japanese culture. His father rented Japanese movies, mostly historical epics. Andy enjoyed these movies, especially those with samurai engaged in spectacular swordfights. But to him, the samurai movies were just like movies about Roman gladiators or American cowboys: they were action pictures, and fun to watch. He didn't see them as being about his ancestors.

On his own, Andy had gone to a number of anime films. He didn't think of these as particularly Japanese, either, though the animation style had originated in Japan. In fact, they had become really popular among all his high school friends.

Now Andy would get to see Japan with his own eyes. At his mother's suggestion, he began to review the Japanese phrases his father had taught him years before. Andy also decided to review different types of Japanese writing, especially katakana, which his father told him was used on public signs.

The whole orchestra worked hard ringing doorbells and washing cars, but as summer approached, they all knew that they still hadn't raised enough money to pay for the tickets. Would the auction bring in enough?

At lunch one day, Andy was sitting at his usual table, next to Sue. The first time he'd come back to sit with her, there had been significant looks and raised eyebrows from Mia and Ginny, but he pretended not to notice. After that, things pretty much went back to the way they were before.

"So, the auction is next Sunday," said Ginny. "I wonder what kinds of things people are going to sell."

"I heard that someone's offering a week in his family's beach cabin," said Sue.

That beach cabin had been the setting for a lot of Andy's daydreams over the past couple of months. He didn't know what it would go for, but he had about fifty dollars left in his savings account from working the summer before. He wondered what his parents would think if he made a bid for the beach cabin. Probably nothing good.

"It's weird that the items are so different. I mean, one woman's offering some ink painting she made herself!" said Ginny. "How can that compare with tickets to a Seahawks game?"

Andy could feel Sue stiffen next to him. "Well, different people like different things, Ginny," he said. "Take my dad, for instance. He likes black-and-white ink paintings a lot more than tickets to some football game." He turned to Sue and smiled at her. After a second, she smiled back.

The auction took place in the gym. A potluck dinner was served, and the parents of the players brought the food. Andy's mother brought a big platter of teriyaki beef and chicken.

Again, the gym was packed by the time the Suzukis arrived. This time, the gym was crowded not only with families of the players, but also with people who were interested in bidding for some of the items. A line had formed for the food, and many people were already holding plates and eating.

Andy looked over the platters on the long table and

wondered which dish was Mrs. Hua's. Not one of the various salads, he decided, nor a pie or a cake. He spotted a big plate of fried noodles with a brownish color that had certainly come from soy sauce. *I bet that's Mrs. Hua's contribution,* he thought. He pointed the dish out to his father. "Check it out, Dad. I know how much you love fried noodles."

"I'd better get some before it's all gone," agreed his father, pushing his way to the noodle dish.

All right, thought Andy. *Now what if I let Dad know that the noodles were brought by Sue's mother? That might break the ice.* Andy watched his dad, remembering how red his face had gotten when he'd talked about his trip to Beijing. *Yeah, right,* he thought. *Like it's going to be that simple.*

Either way, he didn't get a chance to tell his dad who'd brought the noodles. The eating didn't take long, because people practically inhaled the food. After a few minutes, a tinkling sound interrupted the chatter. Mrs. Fulton, the woman who had chaired the fund-raising program, was rapping a water pitcher with a spoon. "Ladies and gentlemen," she shouted. "Now the fun part begins. Let's start the auction!"

People began to seat themselves on the benches. When it got quiet again, the items to be auctioned off were brought out and put on the refreshment table. Slips of paper describing the service items were neatly arranged in a pile.

Mrs. Fulton picked up a slip and opened the bidding on a pair of tickets to a Seahawks game. Having your lawn mowed for a month was offered next; the winning bid was seventy-five dollars. Personally, Andy thought that the overweight man who won the bidding could have used the exercise, instead of letting someone else do the mowing.

The beach cabin came up for bidding, and before Andy could ever open his mouth, the bidding topped what he could afford. It finally went for five hundred dollars to a man sitting two rows down. So much for his daydreams.

Next the items on the table began to be auctioned off. Andy was surprised that an old Coke bottle was offered as an antique, and went for twenty-five dollars. After a while his attention began to wander. He had little interest in antique maps, china vases, or other junk. He glanced at Sue, thinking about his dream of the week at the beach cabin. Maybe they could go camping some weekend? *Maybe . . .*

Then something made him sit up. His father's voice, making a bid! Andy looked up and saw that the item offered was Sue's mother's ink painting, which lay partially unrolled on the table. His father made an offer of a hundred dollars!

There was a murmur of surprise. Nobody else made an offer, so the painting went to Andy's father. He went down to the auction table, picked up the scroll, and walked back beaming to his seat.

Andy didn't even listen to the rest of the auction as he watched his father slowly unrolling the rest of the painting. Andy could make out a black-and-white brush painting of a landscape, with mountains and a small boat in the foreground. "Better roll up the picture, Don," advised Andy's mother. "Somebody might bump into it and crumple it."

Andy's father slowly rolled up the scroll and tied it with the silk strings that were attached to the two wooden rollers.

Soon the auction was over, and cheers and applause broke out. People slowly began making their way to the exits. Andy searched the audience and spotted Sue with her parents.

Before Andy could make a move, his father was already pushing his way through the crowd toward Sue's family. He must have remembered Mrs. Hua from their last meeting at the gym.

Mrs. Hua looked up and smiled at Andy's father. "You are the gentleman who bought my painting!"

Andy's father smiled back. "Yes, when I heard that you did brush paintings, I had been hoping that one of your pictures would be in the auction. It seems that fortune favored me. Maybe I was virtuous in my previous life!"

Andy knew the Buddhist belief that being virtuous in a previous life led to one's good fortune. Apparently it was an idea that was familiar to the Huas as well. Mrs. Hua looked delighted. "Yes, I can well believe that!"

"Do you do calligraphy work, too?" asked Andy's father.

"I do," said Mrs. Hua. "It's closely related to painting, I always think." She turned to Sue. "You should practice harder with your brush."

"I tried to make my sons practice brushwork, but

they never went beyond writing their names in characters," said Andy's mother.

"They complain that they're too busy with their homework and practicing," agreed Mrs. Hua. "But certain things are more important than others, and proper brush writing is one of the most important!"

"I couldn't agree with you more!" said Andy's father.

Andy's eyes met Sue's, and he knew they were thinking the same thing. This was a good start. Maybe their families could actually become friends!

Rochelle, who had been talking to a group of boys in another corner of the gym, now came over. When she saw the two families standing together, she smiled. "So you did introduce Dad and Mom to Andy's family, after all," she said to Sue.

Mrs. Hua looked bewildered. "No, Sue didn't introduce us." She turned to look at Andy. "You are Sue's friend?"

"We both play in the orchestra," Sue said quickly.

Mr. Hua moved forward. "Perhaps we should introduce ourselves, then," he said. "My name is Samuel Hua, and this is my wife, Lillian. I guess you know our two daughters already."

Andy's mother moved into the circle. She stared at Andy and then turned to the Huas. "No, we have not had a chance to know your two daughters," she said slowly.

The color in Andy's father's face was rising. "Hua? Did you say your name was Hua? That's a Chinese name, isn't it?"

Mrs. Hua nodded. "Yes, we are Chinese, of course.

You're Chinese, too, aren't you? You recognized the painting as being in the Song dynasty style."

"I thought the painting was Japanese," murmured Andy's father, suddenly looking uncomfortable. "Japanese literati artists do black-and-white ink paintings like this."

"You are Japanese?" cried Mrs. Hua.

"And your name is . . . ," said Mr. Hua.

"Our name is Suzuki," said Andy's father. He turned to Andy's mother. "Come on, we have to go home. It's late."

Andy glanced sadly back at Sue as he followed his parents out of the gym. *Guess that was too good to be true.* The only ray of hope was the sight of his father's hand tightly clutching the painting.

They drove home in total silence. As soon as they entered the house, Andy's mother spoke. "I've always found you to be honest with us, Andy. I must say that I'm very disappointed with your underhanded behavior."

"Underhanded?" Andy turned in surprise. "What do you mean?"

"Sneaking off to see a Chinese girl!" cried his father. "You knew perfectly well that we wouldn't approve!"

"I wasn't exactly being *underhanded* about it," protested Andy. "I never snuck off to see Sue. In fact, I really meant to bring Sue over and introduce her. I just . . . never got the chance." Andy couldn't bring himself to say that he was too afraid that his father might offend Sue.

"You just never got the courage!" snapped his father.

"It's not totally a matter of courage," Andy said, trying to be diplomatic. "I just . . . I didn't want her feelings to be hurt."

His mother looked startled. "What do you mean? Do you think I'd insult her if she visited us?"

"No, *you* wouldn't," said Andy quickly, looking nervously at his father. "But I didn't want Sue to hear Dad talk about how dirty and backward the Chinese are, or how people spit in the streets."

There was silence. Andy's father threw himself on the sofa in the living room and picked up the newspaper. He turned the front page so violently that it tore. He then threw the paper on the floor and glowered.

Andy's mother went into the kitchen and came back a few minutes later with cups of tea. As far back as Andy could remember, whenever there was a stormy scene at home, his mother served tea, the soothing drink that was supposed to calm tempers. This time its soothing effect didn't work right away. Father and son both sat in stony silence, not meeting each other's eye.

Finally Andy's mother broke the silence. "Andy, I don't think you're being quite fair to your father. If you brought a guest home, your father would never insult her to her face. *You're* the one who is insulting. You insult your father if you believe that he would behave in such a manner."

"Well, he might not insult her on purpose," said Andy, "but inside, he would still think of Sue as a backward, dirty Chinese. What if something slipped out and she found out how he really feels?" *Especially if Dad glowered at her like that.*

"Don, I think you should take a wider view," said his mother, turning to Andy's father. "Instead of thinking about the man who spat on your shoe and yelled at you—"

"That's the trouble with you historians! You take such a wide view that you can't see the nose in front of your face!"

"What did I fail to see?" demanded Andy's mother.

"A little detail such as our son sneaking off to see a girl he knows we won't approve of!" said his father.

"Come on," protested Andy. "I wasn't sneaking off. I was just waiting for the right moment to introduce you to Sue." After a moment, he added sadly, "But I see now that it's hopeless."

Another silence. Then Andy's mother sighed. "Andy, you have a low opinion of me if you don't believe that I can change your father's mind about the Chinese."

"Now wait a minute!" demanded Andy's father. "Just what makes you think you can change my mind?"

Andy looked at his mother and saw that she was smiling. "I can start by mentioning the painting you bought," she said.

His father looked embarrassed. "I . . . I was mistaken, that's all. I thought the painting was Japanese."

"And what made you think the painting was Japanese?" asked Andy's mother.

"Well . . . the style . . . it's black-and-white . . . the brushstrokes . . ."

"I know, it's in the literati style, the kind that you especially like, isn't it?" continued his mother. "And where did the literati artists get their inspiration?"

"All right, all right!" muttered Andy's father. "So those artists learned the style from the Chinese. Maybe the Chinese were cultured people at one time. . . ."

"They taught the Japanese how to write," said Andy out of the side of his mouth.

But his father heard him anyway. "That was more than a thousand years ago! The man who spat on my shoe, he's someone who lives in China *today*!"

"Mrs. Hua didn't live a thousand years ago," said Andy's mother. "She's a living, breathing Chinese—well, okay, a Chinese American. I personally would like to get acquainted with her. And with her family."

Andy waited anxiously. His father took a deep breath, and after a minute the red in his face began to fade.

His mother then said, "Why don't we invite your friend—what was her name again? Oh yes, Sue—to our house?"

Andy's father frowned. He seemed to be considering the idea. Andy wondered whether he was picturing Sue dumping garbage everywhere and spitting on his shoes. After a moment his father nodded. "Oh, all right. Maybe we can give her a few tips on what to expect in Japan. There are things she has to know for the orchestra trip."

Andy felt a rush of relief, but it quickly gave way to concern when he remembered what Sue had told him about her mother and grandmother. "Uh . . . well . . . the thing is . . ."

"What's the matter, Andy?" his mother asked quietly.

Andy said in a rush, "Honestly, I'm not sure how

Sue's parents will feel about her visiting a Japanese family."

His father's face reddened again, and Andy knew that the little bit of ground he had gained was lost. He just hoped his mother would be able to smooth things over one more time.

6

As the Huas made their way home, Rochelle was the only person who said anything.

"What did I tell you, Sue? You should have let Dad and Mom know about Andy!"

Sue didn't reply. They sat in icy silence for the rest of the drive.

When they arrived home, Sue went into the kitchen to make some tea. Whenever there was a stormy scene at home, her mother always served tea, a soothing drink that was supposed to calm tempers. But this time its soothing effect didn't work right away.

Her mother took a sip of tea, found it too hot, and

banged her cup down. She glared at Sue. "To think that you would become friendly with one of those monsters! How could you betray your grandmother like this?"

Sue tightened her lips. She had known that her grandmother's feelings would be hurt by learning that she was seeing a Japanese boy, but to call it a betrayal was unfair. She didn't say anything, though, not wanting to make things worse. She would just have to ride out the storm.

Rochelle looked uncomfortable. "Mom, Andy isn't a monster," she said. "He plays the violin. From what I hear, he's pretty good, too."

Her mother's lips curled. "Ha! So you think that playing the violin excuses everything? Didn't some evil Roman emperor play the violin while the city burned?"

"Nero didn't play the violin," murmured Sue. "It wasn't even invented yet. People think that what he played must have been a lyre."

"Don't try to be smart with me, young lady!" shouted her mother. "It's not just that the boy is Japanese. What I can't forgive is your dishonesty, your sneaky behavior."

Sue's father put down his teacup gently on the coffee table. "Lillian, I think you're not being fair to Sue." He turned to Sue. "I gather that you didn't tell us about this boy because you knew we would disapprove?"

Sue's throat tightened. She was prepared to face her mother's anger, but her father's sympathy almost broke her down. She took a deep breath and cleared her throat. "I didn't mean to hide Andy from you forever. I just wanted to wait until I got the chance to convince you that not all Japanese are monsters."

"You'll have a long, long wait!" snapped her mother. "The Japanese *are* monsters, and waiting for them to change their true nature will take more time than you've got!"

"But Andy's an American!" protested Sue. "He grew up in this country! He's as American as Rochelle and me!"

Her mother sneered. "You are a *Chinese* American. Unless you want to dye your hair and get an operation to change the shape of your eyes, you will never be one hundred percent American. But even that won't change your true nature. That boy is a *Japanese* American, and nothing will change his true nature, either."

Sue was beginning to grow angry. "Not all the people in a country have the same nature! Look around you: not all Americans are exactly alike!"

"Lillian," said Sue's father, "Sue has a point there. You can't generalize. Every country has its monsters and its saints."

"So this Japanese boy—pardon me, this Japanese *American* boy—is now a saint?" asked her mother. "The result of living in America, no doubt?"

"Come, come, Lillian. Living in America does change people. We've changed ourselves." Her father tried to inject some humor. "Why, I've even seen you put ketchup on some French fries!"

The attempt at humor was a mistake. Sue's mother was now almost panting with rage. "Then this trip to Japan would bring out his true Japanese nature again and wipe out the civilizing effect of living in America! I don't think we should let Sue go. I never liked the idea of her going in the first place. But I know how much the orchestra means to her, so I didn't try to stop her from going. Now I see that the trip would have a disastrous effect on her true nature!"

"Mom, that's not fair!" objected Rochelle. "After Sue worked so hard to help raise money!"

Sue's heart was in her throat. Could her mother really forbid her to go on the trip? Would her father be able to talk her mother around?

Apparently he was going to try. "Lillian, Rochelle's mention of raising money for the trip reminds me of the auction. Remember who made the bid for your painting?"

Sue's mother gaped. She closed her mouth and took a breath. "Well, he only picked it because he thought it was a Japanese painting," she said finally.

"He picked it because he has good taste," said Sue's father. "He has a discriminating eye."

Sue wanted to give her father a big hug. But she didn't, because emotional displays embarrassed him. She admired his cleverness. He knew that the way to reach her mother was through her artwork. Besides, he had told the simple truth. Mr. Suzuki had chosen her mother's painting because he had admired it.

"Sue," said her father. "Can we have some fresh tea? Mine is getting cold and bitter."

Sue went into the kitchen to put the electric kettle on. As she rinsed the old leaves out of the teapot and put a fresh batch in, she could hear her father asking her mother and Rochelle to sit down. "I've got something to tell you, but let's wait until Sue is back."

When Sue had poured everyone a fresh cup of hot tea and joined the others in the living room, her father cleared his throat. "We had a retired member in our department, another art historian. His name was Hideo Hasegawa." He paused to take a sip of his tea. "As you know, we've socialized with most of the people in our department. We've been invited to their homes, and we've invited them back."

Sue remembered that her parents had invited a number of faculty members for dinner. Rochelle had even flirted with some of the younger ones. But she didn't remember ever seeing someone called Hasegawa at their house. With her mother's hatred of the Japanese, she could understand why he had never been invited.

Her father continued. "I saw very little of Hasegawa. The retired professors still have offices at the university, but they don't come regularly. I'd also heard that Professor Hasegawa was not in good health. Then one day we had a guest speaker, an expert on fifteenth-century Flemish art, which of course is my own specialty. After the talk, the department gave a dinner party for the speaker at a local restaurant. I decided to attend because I wanted a chance to talk some more with the speaker. To my surprise, Hasegawa was also at the dinner. In fact, we were seated next to each other at the table."

"They probably thought you were close friends, since you were both Asians," muttered Sue's mother. For once Sue didn't think her mother was exaggerating.

"We started talking," continued her father. "I soon found out that he was also interested in Flemish art, although he specialized in a slightly later period. In fact, we shared quite a few interests."

"But you didn't invite him home," murmured Sue.

Her father glanced briefly at her mother. "No," he said. "But after that, I began to drop by his office to chat whenever he was on campus. He also came to my office a few times, and eventually, we started going to the campus cafeteria for an occasional afternoon snack."

Sue wanted to smile. She was picturing her father and Professor Hasegawa sneaking off for a bite at Hero's.

Her father continued. "I forget how we got on the subject of wars. Probably it started when we discussed the looting of European art by the Nazis. I talked about how destructive wars were."

Sue glanced over at her mother. She knew how fiercely opposed to war her mother was, and that she had taken part in many antiwar demonstrations. On a couple of occasions she had even taken Rochelle and Sue along. She stopped doing that when the girls had been almost trampled underfoot in one of the demonstrations that had gotten out of hand. Her mother's antiwar activities had stirred Sue's interest in the history of warfare.

"So I told Hasegawa about my wife taking part in antiwar movements," her father went on. "When I said this, I noticed that Hasegawa's face became rigid. It was obviously an extremely painful subject for him. Finally he asked me whether my wife had ever been arrested, and when I told him that she had not, the conversation ended."

"Why was it painful for him?" asked Sue's mother. Her voice came out a little husky, and she had to clear her throat. "Did he tell you?"

"Not that day, nor the next," replied Sue's father. "But a week later, he came to my office and told me his story. When he was a college student in Japan, he spoke out openly against the militaristic actions of the army, and against the invasion of China. Some of his neighbors reported his remarks to the authorities, and Hasegawa was arrested."

"I guess I was luckier," Sue's mother said softly.

"You were *much* luckier," said Sue's father. "Hasegawa was released at the end of the war, but his health never fully recovered from the harsh prison conditions. He later immigrated to America, because he could not bear to live in the same place as the neighbors who had informed on him."

There was a long silence. Then Sue's father spoke again. "Hasegawa also told me that he was not alone in opposing the actions of the Japanese government. There were many people who felt as he did, but the ones who spoke out wound up in prison."

"But surely it wasn't a secret that there were people opposed to the war?" asked Sue's mother.

"You should know better than anybody that governments don't always listen to protesters."

"What happened to him after he moved to America?" asked Sue.

"He continued his education at an American university, and after he got his degree, he found a teaching job, got married, and raised a family here."

"Sounds like a happy ending," said Rochelle. "Maybe it's not too late to invite Professor Hasegawa to our house."

"I'm afraid it *is* too late," replied her father. "Professor Hasegawa died last year."

Sue saw the keen regret on her father's face, and she felt the same way. If her mother had met the Hasegawa family, her ideas about the Japanese might have changed.

After another silence, Sue's mother nodded and said, "So the moral of your story is that not all the Japanese are the same, right?"

"Let's give them a chance before we rush to judgment," said Sue's father.

Sue relaxed. She knew now that her mother would at least agree to meet Andy.

When Sue joined Andy in line for lunch next day, she could tell immediately that he had also made peace with his parents. There was a brightness in his face as he looked at her, and his eyebrows danced the way they did when he was playing a piece of music he enjoyed.

She smiled at him and told him about the scene that had taken place in her living room. "My father told us about this Japanese professor who was imprisoned because he opposed his country's invasion of China. That convinced my mom that not all the Japanese are the same."

Andy grinned. "I'm glad I don't have to show her my grandfather's Purple Heart, then."

"So how did you convince your father to let you date a backward, spitting Chinese girl?" asked Sue.

"I think what swayed him was your mom's painting," said Andy. "He really likes it, even after he found out it was painted by a Chinese woman."

Sue finally knew the real meaning of the phrase "a full heart." Hers threatened to burst with happiness.

"Hey, lovebirds," Mia's voice said, "I know you plan to spend the day in line gazing into each other's eyes. But the rest of us have to get lunch, too."

At the start of the next rehearsal, Mr. Baxter looked gravely around at his orchestra members and said, "Folks, there's something I've got to tell you."

Andy's heart sank. He had been dreading this. All that doorbell ringing and car washing had been for nothing!

Suddenly Mr. Baxter broke into a huge grin. "After adding up the money made from the auction, the door-to-door campaign, and the car washing, it looks like we've got enough to get tickets for everybody. Our trip is on!"

The players broke out into cheers. Andy began to tap his music stand with his bow, as violinists do to show their delight. Soon all the other string players followed suit. The French horns boomed, the trumpets blared, the oboes bleated, and the flutes gurgled.

Later that week, Andy invited Sue to go to the jazz concert with him, and she accepted. When he came to her house to pick her up, he thought she looked a little nervous as she answered the door.

"My grandmother's visiting tonight," she told him.

"Okay, I won't push my luck by coming in, then," said Andy. Sue's mother might be willing to give him a chance, but he knew her grandmother was a different story.

A week later, Andy took Sue to see an anime movie, and they ran into Rochelle and Jake afterward. The four of them went to Burger King together.

"So are you looking forward to Tokyo?" Rochelle asked Andy.

"Looking forward, but also a little scared," said Andy. When they heard his name was Suzuki, the Japanese would expect a lot from him. The thought made his stomach twist. It was like getting ready to play a solo recital.

"Yeah, I'll bet you're scared, with Godzilla over there just waiting to stomp on you," said Jake.

Andy relaxed and smiled. "I think I could take Godzilla. Tokyo, here we come!"

As instructed, Sue and her family arrived at the airport two hours before the Tokyo flight was supposed to depart. It seemed that most of the other orchestra members and their families were already there. Sue joined the check-in line and found herself standing behind Mia.

"Hey, Sue!" said Mia. "Aren't you psyched? I couldn't sleep at all last night!"

"Me neither," said Sue, although that wasn't entirely true. She had actually slept for about two hours. She hoped to make up the rest on the plane. "I remember that when I went to Hong Kong six years ago, I had really bad jet lag. I woke up at two AM on my first morning there."

Mia groaned. "I don't want to hear about it!"

"But I got over it pretty fast," Sue reassured Mia. "By the second morning, I was waking up at five o'clock."

"Enough!" cried Mia.

It took about half an hour for Sue to get checked in, and with more than an hour to kill before boarding time, her mother suggested going to the coffee shop. At least they would be able to sit down, instead of standing around. Standing for so long was tiring for Grandma Mei.

"I want to see my precious granddaughter before she embarks on this dangerous journey into enemy territory," declared Grandma Mei.

Sue sighed. Her classmates probably thought Grandma was kidding, but Sue knew she wasn't. The coffee shop was packed. The other orchestra members and their parents were killing time as well. At one table, several people got up to leave, and the Huas quickly moved over to grab the four empty seats. But their party of five still needed one more.

"I can move over a little, and you can squeeze in another chair," said a familiar voice.

The speaker was Andy. Sue was so dazed and excited, she hadn't even noticed him there. Sitting with him were his parents. They stared openmouthed at the new arrivals. Sue's parents stood motionless. Although Andy and Sue had been dating openly, the two sets of parents had not met after the auction.

"How kind of you," said Grandma Mei, and immediately sat in one of the empty chairs.

It was as if someone had punched a release button. The two families, the Huas and the Suzukis, started moving. Andy brought over a chair from another table, and everyone found a seat.

"Shall I get some tea and muffins?" asked Sue's father. Without waiting for an answer, he nimbly escaped from the table and went over to the counter to place the order.

Mr. Suzuki cleared his throat. "I'm really enjoying your painting," he said formally to Sue's mother. "I'm hanging it up in the living room."

Sue's mother found her voice. "Thank you."

Grandma Mei beamed with pleasure. "So you like brush paintings?" she asked Mr. Suzuki.

"Very much!" said Mr. Suzuki. "I especially like black-and-white paintings. It's closely related to brush calligraphy."

"Good, good," said Grandma Mei. "These days, so few people develop a skill in brush calligraphy!"

Please don't ask to be introduced, Sue prayed silently. Her grandmother must have assumed that Mr. Suzuki was Chinese, since he had the good taste to admire black-and-white brush paintings. Sue crossed her fingers. *Just don't ask this guy his name!*

Grandma Mei turned to look at Andy. "And you are a member of the orchestra as well?"

Andy was practically bowing. Grandma Mei had that effect on people. "Yes, ma'am, I'm a violinist."

This also earned a wide smile of approval from Grandma Mei. "I'm so glad to hear that! Some people claim that sports develop character, but I have always believed that music is even more demanding, and good for character building."

"I practice very hard, ma'am," said Andy, looking so angelic that Sue could imagine a halo floating above his head.

"Oh, there you are!" said Mia, coming into the coffee shop. "Mr. Baxter says it's getting close to boarding time. He wants all of us gathered in front of the security checkpoint."

Sue and her family quickly got up from the table. As she left the coffee shop, Sue felt a certain relief. Grandma Mei hadn't had time to learn that their companions' name was Suzuki. Sue couldn't imagine how her grandmother might have reacted if she had. As she walked toward the gate, Sue felt alternately a flutter of excitement about the coming trip and a tightness in her chest at the thought of being separated from her family by thousands of miles.

Since only passengers were allowed to go to the departure gate, the people seeing them off had to say goodbye in front of the security checkpoint. Sue's mother gave her a hug that squeezed all the air from her lungs.

Even her father, not a demonstrative person, gave her a tight hug.

Rochelle handed Sue her viola case, which she had been holding. "You think the orchestra can use an extra violin, if I promise to play very, very softly?"

Grandma Mei wiped her eyes and kissed Sue's cheek. "You'll do just fine, Sue. I know you will."

As Sue turned toward the gate, she found Andy beside her.

"We're seated in different rows," he said. "But once we're in the air, we can probably switch with somebody."

"I guess you and your boyfriend's families finally met," said Mia, coming up behind them.

Grandma Mei, who was just about to walk away, turned back. She smiled at Sue. "So this is your boyfriend? Good, good! You've always been a shy girl, but you found a nice boy in the end."

"Looks like you were worrying for no reason at all," continued Mia. "See? Chinese and Japanese families can get along fine!"

Grandma Mei's smile faded. "What did you say? What's this about Chinese and Japanese families?"

Mia covered her mouth. "Oops! Did I just say something I wasn't supposed to?"

Sue took a deep breath and faced her grandmother. She knew the time had come to be honest with her. "Andy's last name is Suzuki, Grandma. He and his family are Japanese Americans."

Grandma Mei said nothing. For a minute Sue

thought that her grandmother had not heard her. Her still face looked more than ever like a dried persimmon. It was white with powder, and the lines in her skin ran deep. But her eyes that stared at Sue glittered, and they were sharp enough to cut glass.

Sue had the feeling that she and her grandmother faced each other alone in the busy airport. Mia had immediately escaped, and the Suzuki family had also gone to join the other students and their families. Even Sue's parents and Rochelle seemed to be distant.

"I have always loved you, Sue, because I thought you were a true Chinese lady," said Grandma Mei. She did not raise her voice, but that made her even scarier. "What I have admired most in you was your honesty."

"Grandma, I haven't really told you any lies about Andy," Sue began. She stopped, knowing that the argument was weak.

Grandma Mei went on as if she hadn't heard Sue. "But your scheme, your plot to make me meet your boyfriend and his family, that's contemptible!"

"Mother, it was not a plot!" cried Sue's mother. "It was a pure accident!"

"Grandma, you're not being fair to Sue!" protested Rochelle almost at the same time.

"Go!" Grandma Mei said to Sue. "Go to Japan! That's where you truly want to be!"

She turned and marched off. Sue's parents gave her quick hugs and ran after Grandma Mei.

Mr. Baxter's voice rose above the murmur of the crowd. "Come on, folks, we've got to get a move on!"

As she hurried toward the security checkpoint, Sue could still picture the expression on Grandma Mei's face. It was not just anger. Sue could cope with that. What she also saw was sadness, and that tore at her heart.

7

Andy felt light-headed by the time the plane finally landed at Narita Airport. During the nine-hour flight he'd hardly been able to sleep at all. All of a sudden, he was completely freaked out by two things: one, that Japan might not live up to what he hoped to see, and two (this was the one that worried him more, if he was being honest with himself), that he might not live up to what the Japanese expected of him. He hated the idea of making a terrible impression and shaming his family.

As the plane began its circling descent, he looked down at Sue, whose head was resting on his shoulder. While he had been psyching himself out about what might go wrong in Tokyo, Sue had managed to doze off more than once. He couldn't help smiling down at her as her breath gently stirred the shiny curtain of hair that covered half her face.

After a while, she began to stir. "How are you doing?" he asked gently.

Sue yawned and rubbed her eyes. "Not bad. I must have slept a couple of hours, I think. How 'bout you?"

"Maybe I dozed between movies," he lied. "I should have turned the headphones off and tried to get some rest, but I couldn't really sleep much. Too nervous, I guess."

Finally, with a huge bump, the plane touched down on the runway. Andy sat impatiently as the plane taxied to the gate. It seemed to take forever, but the plane finally stopped, there was a *beep,* and the seat belt sign went off. People began to move. Andy got up and retrieved his violin from the overhead compartment. The doors were opened, and he and Sue picked up their backpacks and followed the crowd. Andy's legs felt like rubber. After that long trip, he couldn't get out of the plane fast enough.

But at the same time he wasn't quite ready to set his foot on Japanese land—the land where his ancestors had come from. He took a deep breath and stepped through the door of the plane. Now he was *really* in Japan.

But the terminal looked just like any other airport terminal. Many of the signs were even in English, Andy noted with disappointment. Feeling slightly deflated, he followed the other Lakeview kids through the immigration line. That didn't take long, since the whole orchestra passed through as one party.

The wait for their luggage was tedious, and then they had to go through customs. It took even longer than usual because they had to wait for everybody in their party. Finally, about an hour or so after they'd landed, they were out.

Waiting for them just outside customs was a big crowd of Japanese people. Andy guessed they were their host families. Mr. Baxter walked over to meet a middle-aged Japanese man, who Andy remembered as the Kasei School's orchestra conductor. Andy couldn't help contrasting the Japanese man, who wore a neat suit and tie, with Mr. Baxter, who wore a rumpled T-shirt and jeans. Andy realized that he must look pretty rumpled, too. He hoped his host family wouldn't hold it against him.

Mr. Baxter began to read out the names of the orchestra members, and after each name was read, the school representative read out the name of the host family. Andy saw that some of the orchestra members were greeted warmly by Japanese students he recognized from the Kasei School's visit. Some of his fellow orchestra members were being reunited with the Japanese players they had hosted.

Andy heard Sue's name being read, and then the name Chong. Andy frowned. That wasn't a Japanese name. Sue had just joined the orchestra this year, so she wouldn't know any of the Japanese players and would be staying with strangers. Sue smiled nervously and gave Andy a little wave, then went off to join a serious-looking middle-aged couple.

Andy would also be staying with strangers. He had to

wait a long time before he was called, since their names were in alphabetical order. Finally, he heard his name, followed by the name Sato. A short, middle-aged couple and a teenage girl stepped forward to greet him.

The Satos looked about the same age as Andy's own parents. Mr. and Mrs. Sato were the exact same height, which was more than a head shorter than Andy. The daughter was a little taller than her parents, but not much, and she looked as slender as a blade of grass. Looming over the family, Andy felt like a Kodiak bear.

Andy bowed, and then his mind went blank. With a great effort, he managed to dredge up the phrase he had been rehearsing before leaving home, *"Hajime mashite."* It was the Japanese phrase used when greeting someone for the first time.

Mr. Sato smiled and poured a torrent of Japanese over Andy. Andy blushed. *Great. Now they think I'm fluent.* "Uh . . . I'm afraid my Japanese isn't so good," Andy said, trying to look apologetic.

Mr. Sato abruptly stopped smiling and switched into English. "This is my wife, and this is our daughter, Haruko. Welcome to Japan, Andy-kun."

Andy bowed again, and smiled at Mrs. Sato and Haruko. Mrs. Sato gave a flicker of a smile, while Haruko's face held no expression. Andy couldn't tell whether she was disappointed by him or just bored. He'd never seen such a totally blank face before.

Andy tried to study the girl without being too obvious. She was about the same height as Sue, and both of them had a slim build. There the resemblance ended.

Whereas Sue had long, straight black hair that fell in a shining sheet, Haruko's was cut very short, and bleached a pale blond. But the greatest difference between the two girls was in their expressions. Sue generally looked serious, but Andy could see humor lurking not far from the surface, and he always felt that her smile was on the point of breaking out. Haruko's face held no trace of humor whatsoever.

"We usually take the train from Narita Airport," Mr. Sato told Andy. "But since you must be tired after the trip, we thought we'd drive into Tokyo."

Something in his voice told Andy that driving to and from the airport, the normal thing to do in America, was a big undertaking here and a sacrifice on Mr. Sato's part.

"It's very kind of you to drive me," Andy said quickly. "Thank you very much for going to so much trouble."

Both Mr. and Mrs. Sato smiled at Andy. Apparently he had said the right thing. *Score one for Andy.*

Stepping out of the air-conditioned terminal building and walking into the open air of late July was like being slapped in the face with a slice of hot pizza—the side with the cheese and pepperoni. It had been hot back home, but nothing like this. The humidity made the heat feel a hundred times worse.

Andy plodded after the Satos, carrying his backpack on his back and pulling his wheeled suitcase with one hand while holding his violin case with the other. He could feel the sweat running down his face and into his eyes, almost blinding him. Since his hands were full, he couldn't wipe his eyes. Of course Mr. and Mrs. Sato belonged to an older generation and couldn't be expected to help carry his luggage, but he thought Haruko could have offered to take the violin case, at least. He blinked away some sweat from his eyes and stole a look at her. She glanced coldly at him and turned her head away. *What is with her?*

At last they reached the garage where the car was parked. As Mr. Sato unlocked the Toyota, Andy wondered how they were going to fit him and his luggage in. Back home, his family also drove a Toyota, but it was much bigger than the Satos' car. He didn't realize that Toyota made a model as teeny as this one. It seemed like a golf cart to him.

The trunk did hold Andy's suitcase and violin case. He got in—inserted himself into—the backseat with Haruko, shoving his backpack in before him. She winced as she sat down beside him, and Andy wondered if he smelled bad. After all, he'd been on a plane for nine hours, and it was pretty hot outside. It was a blessing when Mr. Sato started the engine and turned the air-conditioning on.

Andy couldn't tell how long it took to drive into Tokyo, because he dozed during most of the trip. At first he tried hard to stay awake. After they left the airport, they drove past some fields. Andy saw old-fashioned Japanese houses with sloping tiled roofs. It was almost like seeing a costume movie. He wanted to ask about the countryside, but he was swamped by a wave of sleepiness. He woke up a little later and saw that they were driving on a freeway that had walls on either side, obscuring the view, so he lost interest.

The next time he opened his eyes, he saw that they had left the freeway and were driving through a city street. The street was so narrow that it barely had room for one car. Pedestrians had no sidewalks, only a narrow path along the side of the road, which was marked off by a white stripe or a low metal railing. Andy wondered how a big fat sumo wrestler would avoid being scraped by a passing car.

"We're almost there," said Mr. Sato.

A few minutes later, they stopped, turned into a driveway, and parked under a carport made of transparent brown plastic. After the Satos got out, Andy struggled from the car, stood up, and looked around. Suddenly he was overwhelmed by the differences from Seattle.

This is Japan, the land my ancestors came from. But it looks so alien! The neighborhood was a residential one, and yet he couldn't see the other houses, because they were all surrounded by a tall fence that hid almost everything except the roof. It looked forbidding and unfriendly, so different from his street back home.

Mrs. Sato opened a gate by the side of the carport and beckoned Andy to follow. He picked up his luggage, passed through the gate, and found himself in a small courtyard. A path of irregularly shaped stepping-stones led to the house. In front of him, Mr. Sato and Haruko were already mounting the stairs leading into the house.

Once they entered, the Satos removed their shoes. Removing his shoes before entering the house was something Andy also did at home. He quickly followed their example. Stepping up into the house, he placed his shoes on a shelf in the same cabinet used by the others. His shoes were a couple of inches longer than the next biggest pair, those belonging to Mr. Sato, and they stuck out so much that he couldn't close the cabinet door. *Oh well, at least all the shoes will get a good airing.*

Mrs. Sato handed Andy a pair of plastic slippers. Mr. Sato and Haruko were already shuffling off. Andy obediently put the slippers on. He found them slightly clammy.

"I show you to your room," Mrs. Sato told Andy.

Shuffling along the dark wooden floor of a narrow corridor, Andy followed his hostess to the end of the hall, where she slid open a door and beckoned him to enter.

It was a tiny room, almost a cell, but it had a desk with a lamp, a standing wooden wardrobe, and a narrow cot. Andy, who was pretty narrow himself, was not worried about the width of the cot. It was its length that was a problem.

Mrs. Sato realized the same. She looked him up and down and then turned her eyes to the cot. "Maybe you too long?" she murmured.

"Too long," Andy agreed.

"Can you sleep on floor?" she asked.

"Of course I can!" declared Andy. He had been expecting to sleep on the floor anyway. On camping trips he had slept in a sleeping bag spread out on the hard ground. "I bring futon," said Mrs. Sato, and hurried out.

Andy decided to use the cot as a shelf for his belongings. He put his violin and suitcase on the cot and began to unpack. By the time he had emptied his suitcase, his belongings filled the whole cot.

Among the things he took out was a big box of smoked salmon, which was a local specialty at home. His mother had bought the salmon for him to present to his host family. She had told him that in Japan, you were expected to bring *meibutsu,* local specialty, as a gift.

Mrs. Sato staggered in, carrying what looked like a big folded mattress. In Seattle, some of Andy's friends had futons, but the American version had a bulky wooden frame and looked more or less like a couch that folded. Here, it seemed, a futon was just a mattress. As Mrs. Sato struggled with it, Andy bent down to help. *Haruko's not lifting a finger to help her mother with the houseguest,* he noted.

Once the futon was on the floor, Andy presented the box of salmon to her with a little bow. Her eyes widened in surprise. Apparently she hadn't expected him to be so civilized. She poured out her thanks in Japanese, and Andy blushed and made some modest-sounding murmurs. That seemed to be the right response, and Andy felt his stock rising.

Andy's next need, an urgent one, was to use the toilet. *"Obenjo?"* he asked. It was one of the vitally important terms his parents had insisted he learn.

Mrs. Sato stared for a moment, and then said, *"Toire?"*

Apparently the word for "toilet" that his parents

had taught him was no longer used, and the word used these days was "toire." Of course! "Toire" was simply the English word "toilet," modified a little. Andy nodded eagerly. He followed Mrs. Sato down the hallway and came to a door, which she slid open.

"Slippers!" she ordered.

Andy saw a pair of slippers inside the toilet and realized that he had to take off the slippers he had put on at the front door and put on these special toilet slippers. *When in Rome,* he thought, and did as Mrs. Sato ordered. After he closed the door, he looked around the tiny room. It contained a toilet, and nothing else—no bathing facilities, no sink. On the back of the toilet, however, was a small basin with a faucet, for washing one's hands, obviously.

Andy peered at the toilet and studied it. He prodded the seat, which was soft and made of plastic. It also felt slightly warm, and seemed to be electrically heated. *That might be very welcome in winter,* he thought, but it was a luxury he could do without in July. What caught his attention was a list of choices on the flush mechanism written in Chinese characters. Andy knew some basic characters, so he knew that the choices presented were "big," "small," and "beauty."

He sat down on the soft seat, and after using the toilet he chose "big" for the flush while still seated. A powerful jet of warm water shot up and gave him a thorough wash. *Wow. If even the middle-grade flush is like this, the "beauty" choice must be quite something.* A bit thrown off by his experience, he hurried out of the toilet and headed for his room. Before he had gone more than three steps, he was waylaid by Mrs. Sato.

"Slippers!" she hissed.

Andy realized that in his hurry, he had forgotten to replace the toilet slippers. Blushing with shame, he hurried back, shuffled off the toilet slippers, and slid his feet into his regular slippers. All the points for good behavior that he had earned so far went down the drain—with a "beauty" flush.

Mrs. Sato studied him. "Bath?" she asked.

A bath sounded like heaven. "Yes, please!" he said.

He followed her to another door, which she slid open. The small room inside contained a big square fiberglass tub, about three feet wide and three feet deep. It was covered by a plastic top.

Mrs. Sato folded back the top, and Andy saw that the tub was already more than half full of clean, hot water. Mrs. Sato indicated some faucets in the wall, a small bucket, a soap dish, and some scrubbers made of gourd fiber.

Andy remembered the careful instructions he had received from his parents on how to take a bath in Japan. "I wash first, and after I'm clean, then I enter the bathtub, right?"

Mrs. Sato beamed at him and nodded. Andy smiled back. He had just earned back some points. After she left, Andy lost no time in stripping off his clothes. He splashed himself with water from the taps, soaped himself, and used the scrubber. It felt rather harsh, but it sure did a good job of scraping off the dirt.

After he rinsed himself off completely, Andy dipped his hand cautiously in the tub. The temperature of the water seemed about right for boiling potatoes. He preferred to stay uncooked, so instead of soaking in the tub, he decided to dry himself. The bath towel Mrs. Sato gave him was a thin piece of terry cloth approximately one foot by two, but it was so hot in the room that the skimpy little towel was good enough.

Just as he started to take up his clothes, the door opened, and Mrs. Sato appeared. Andy froze. *Ohmigod. Hostess. I'm naked.* But his hostess seemed to feel that the sight of a naked male body was all in a day's work. "Here is *yukata* for wearing after bath," she said casually, handing him a cotton kimono and a dark, narrow sash. She left the bathroom and slid the door closed behind her.

Andy let his breath out in a whoosh. *That was weird.* Then he remembered his parents' telling him that there were public baths and hot spring resorts in Japan where dozens of strangers bathed together. So he guessed seeing a naked stranger was nothing new. Grinning at his own embarrassment, he wondered if any of the other Lakeview players would get a similar surprise from their hostesses.

Andy hurriedly slipped on the yukata. It felt exactly right for a hot summer day, and was much more comfortable than jeans and a T-shirt. He decided that he would try to buy one of these cotton kimonos to bring home. Without bothering to tie the sash, he clutched the kimono around his waist and stepped cautiously out of the bathroom. His slippers, lined up and facing the right direction, were waiting for him outside the door. So was Mrs. Sato.

She took one look at him and shook her head in disapproval. "Left side on top!" she said.

Andy sighed. What had he done wrong now?

Mrs. Sato pointed at Andy's kimono and repeated, "Left side on top." When he still stared at her in bewilderment, she said, "Only dead people wear right side on top."

Oops. It seemed that how you brought the two parts of the kimono together was important. His stock plummeted again.

Back in his room, he found that Mrs. Sato had unfolded his futon and placed a sheet over it. There was also a folded sheet and a very large terry cloth towel. Andy decided that the large towel was meant as a blanket.

Mrs. Sato had also hung up his suit in the wardrobe. It was thoughtful of her to get the wrinkles out, since he had to wear the suit for the concert. But knowing that she had looked through his things felt a little weird. Was she going to fold his underwear, too?

Andy lay down on the futon and placed the blanket/towel over his middle, figuring he deserved a few minutes of rest. There was an eight-hour difference between Japan and home, so it was really two in the morning for him.

One minute later—or so it seemed—someone was looming over him and insistently ordering him to do something.

He opened his eyes and found Mrs. Sato kneeling next to his futon. "You have to get up, Andy-kun. Dinner is ready!"

Groggy from his deep sleep, Andy managed to sit up. He stared at Mrs. Sato blankly. "Wha—wha—" he croaked.

Mrs. Sato wore an air of great patience. "We eat dinner now."

Andy struggled to stand up. "Do I have time to get dressed?" he asked.

Mrs. Sato frowned. "You can eat dinner wearing yukata. But first, put underwear on."

Andy realized that his yukata had become loose, and that it was obvious he was wearing nothing under it. Another lesson learned. He now knew that the yukata was not a dressing gown you put on after a bath, but a garment you could wear in public.

Dressed decently in underwear and the yukata—with the left side on top—Andy followed the sound of voices and found the Sato family seated around the dining table. In addition to Mr. and Mrs. Sato and Haruko, there was an elderly gentleman. His hair was snowy white, and his eyebrows were so long that they practically covered his eyes.

The old gentleman looked like someone who deserved respect, so Andy bowed as low as he could without actually toppling over. "I'm Suzuki Andrew," he said. He knew from his father that in Japan, the family name came first, before the given name. "It is an honor to meet you."

Apparently he had done the right thing. "This is my

father," Mr. Sato said. The old gentleman smiled, and the rest of the Sato family looked relieved.

Andy was glad they were going to sit around a dining table. He had expected to eat kneeling on the floor in front of a low table. Back home his family had gone to Japanese restaurants where they had to sit on the floor to eat, and after about half an hour, his legs would go numb.

"I'm sorry to keep you all waiting," Andy said. "I fell asleep."

Mr. Sato was understanding. "Jet lag, I know. You young people will get over it quickly."

Andy sat down in the empty seat and contemplated his first real Japanese meal. He was a bit disappointed that it didn't look drastically different from what his mom served at home. The main difference was the state-of-the-art electric rice cooker Mrs. Sato was scooping rice from. Andy's mom had a rice cooker that was five years old, and was much simpler in design. This one had so many panels and dials that it looked like a robot. The only things missing were arms to dish out the rice.

That was done by Mrs. Sato, who scooped rice into bowls and handed them to her father-in-law and her husband, then to Andy, and finally to Haruko and herself. Then the family proceeded to help themselves from the tiny dishes of food in front of each diner. Each person now had four dishes of various sizes and shapes, none of them very large. A piece of broiled fish and some deep-fried prawns were in one of the larger plates, boiled vegetables were in a smaller flat plate, and what Andy recognized as yellow pickled radish sat in a tiny round dish.

Andy picked up his chopsticks and uttered the phrase he had learned from his parents, *"Itadakimasu!"* It meant "I receive."

There was a murmur of surprise from the older Mr. Sato. Andy had earned some points again. Mrs. Sato smiled at him and said, *"Dozo,"* which meant "Please."

Andy suddenly found that he was ravenous. After helping himself to some food from the little dishes in front of him, he fell on his bowl of rice and wolfed it down within seconds. Mrs. Sato refilled it, and Andy quickly emptied it again. He caught the elder Mr. Sato's eyes on him and blushed, but the old man merely smiled. He seemed to approve of a boy with a hearty appetite.

Andy turned to Haruko, who was sitting next to him. She had been completely silent at the table and had barely looked at him. He decided to break the ice—a very thick layer of ice. "I'm a junior at Lakeview High School. What grade are you in at Kasei?"

She just stared at him. *Wow, what is her problem?* Too late, he realized that she might not understand him. Maybe that was why she hadn't addressed him at all. "Uh . . . do you understand English?" he asked.

"Of course I do!" spat Haruko, looking furious. "I've been studying it in school since the fifth grade!"

Her accent was pretty good, a lot better than her parents'. So why hadn't she said anything to him? *She must just be rude.*

Mrs. Sato spoke to her daughter in Japanese. Andy understood only a word or two, but he could make out that she wanted Haruko to be more polite. Haruko lapsed into a frigid silence again.

Andy managed to finish the meal without disgracing himself. He even expressed his appreciation with a phrase learned from his parents, *"Gochisosama deshita,"* meaning "That was a feast."

Old Mr. Sato nodded pleasantly, and Mr. and Mrs. Sato both looked pleased. Even Haruko looked pleasantly surprised. So Andy earned more points. He'd better retire while he was still ahead. "I think I'll try to sleep and get over my jet lag," he told his hosts.

Walking back to his room, he found Haruko heading for her room, which was next to his. "My futon is really comfortable," he said. "Do you sleep on a futon, too?"

Haruko froze again. "I've been sleeping on a regular bed for as long as I remember!"

Andy sighed as he slid open the door to his room. He had lost points again. He wondered if the other Lakeview players were going through the same rigorous examination by their host families.

He wondered how Sue was doing with her host family. God, he missed her!

after her name was called, Sue pulled her suitcase over to her hosts, a tired-looking couple. "Hi," she said nervously. "I'm Sue, Sue Hua."

Both the man and woman broke into warm smiles. They looked about the same age as Sue's parents. She noticed that they were slightly taller than most of the other people at the airport. In fact, the woman was a bit taller than the man.

"We are Mr. and Mrs. Chong," said the woman. She paused. "Your name is Hua? That's Chinese, isn't it?"

"Yes, it is," said Sue. "How about your name, Chong? That sounds Chinese, too."

"It's Korean," said Mr. Chong. He picked up Sue's viola case. "Here, let me take this."

"I guess the school felt that since you are not a *real* American and we are not real Japanese, we would be a suitable host family for you," said Mrs. Chong.

Sue stopped in her tracks. She wasn't sure what to say to that. "Not a real American"? Was Mrs. Chong disappointed? When she glanced over at her hostess, Mrs. Chong's wry smile disarmed her and took some of the sting out of her words. But Sue still wasn't sure what to make of the comment.

Thankfully, both the Chongs spoke good English, especially Mrs. Chong. As they walked through the airport terminal building, Sue asked Mrs. Chong where she had learned her excellent English.

"I studied in America for four years," explained Mrs. Chong. "I was at the New England Conservatory of Music."

Sue was impressed. "What instrument did you study?"

"The violin, chiefly, but I also play the viola," said Mrs. Chong. "You play the viola, don't you? That's what it says in the orchestra list the school gave us."

"Yes. My sister was supposed to play the violin, but she gave it up. I could have played her violin, but by then, I liked the viola so much that I stuck with it."

"The viola does have a wonderful mellow sound, doesn't it?" said Mrs. Chong. "Mozart loved the viola, and his viola quintets are among my favorite pieces."

"Do you have kids playing in the Kasei School Orchestra?" asked Sue.

"Our daughter played cello in the orchestra when it toured the States last year," said Mrs. Chong. "But she graduated, and she's now studying at the Toho School of Music."

Sue had heard of the Toho. She knew that some pretty famous musicians had studied there, including the conductor Seiji Ozawa. "Even though your daughter has already graduated, you still volunteered to be a host?" she asked Mrs. Chong.

"I had such a happy time in America that I wanted this chance to meet some young American."

Sue frowned. "And instead, you wound up with me, a Chinese American," she said, thinking back to what Mrs. Chong had said earlier. She rarely thought of herself as less than American back home, and she wondered whether her hostess felt disappointed.

Mrs. Chong smiled. "To me, you're an American, whatever the Kasei School people think."

So Mrs. Chong's earlier remark about Sue's not being a real American was meant to be a joke.

Sue shifted her backpack, which was beginning to stick to her back. She felt thoroughly confused, and wondered whether it was because of jet lag. Although the terminal building was air-conditioned, it was hotter than the plane.

"We don't have much further to go," said Mr. Chong. "We're taking the train into Tokyo, and the station is just down these escalators over here."

At the station there was a long line for tickets. Sue pulled out her purse and looked inside. Although her father had changed some dollars into Japanese yen for her, Sue's Japanese money was all in the form of bills in denominations of five thousand yen or larger. She tried to calculate how much five thousand yen was worth. Was it about five dollars or fifty?

"Don't worry about the ticket," Mr. Chong said when he saw Sue frowning over her money. "We've bought them already." He held out some tickets and handed one to Sue.

"Thank you very much," Sue said, embarrassed.

Sue had some trouble getting her suitcase through the turnstile, and Mr. Chong had to help her. They reached the platform in good time, and Sue sat down next to Mrs. Chong. Mr. Chong sat across the aisle.

It was a smooth-running electric train, and it went so fast that Sue had only glimpses of the passing scenery. "Is this one of the famous Bullet Trains?" she asked.

"No," said Mr. Chong with a laugh. "The Shinkansen, or Bullet Train, runs only on a few arterial lines. This is a special express, which is faster than a regular express."

In a country as crowded as Japan, trains certainly make sense, thought Sue. Soon the swaying of the train sent her into a doze, and once she opened her eyes to find herself almost in Mrs. Chong's lap. "I'm sorry," she mumbled, and straightened up again.

Mrs. Chong laughed. "That's all right. I've had people fall asleep against me before. Better you than some drunken stranger."

The next thing Sue knew was Mrs. Chong saying in

her ear, "We're about to arrive in Tokyo. Better get your suitcase."

The train was slowing down, and people began to move toward the doors. Sue struggled up, made her way to the rack near the door, and pulled out her suitcase. Its weight seemed to have tripled. Somebody must have replaced her clothes and music scores with bricks.

Now that they had arrived in Tokyo, Sue had been expecting to go to the garage where the Chongs had parked their car, or at least to take a taxi. But Mr. Chong told her they had to get on another train, a commuter line that went to the suburb where they lived.

Unlike the modern train station at the airport, the Tokyo station for the commuter train was hot, crowded, and rather dirty. The passageways were lined with small shops and newsstands, selling food, magazines, and even toiletries. They had to go up and down several escalators before they finally got into the commuter train they wanted. It was very crowded, and at first they couldn't get a seat. After a few stops, the crowd thinned, and they were finally able to sit down. It was a local train, stopping at every station, and the ride seemed to last forever.

By the time they finally reached the Chongs' neighborhood, Sue was dead on her feet. She jumped when Mrs. Chong's voice said in her ear, "Better be prepared. We're getting off at the next stop."

It was a good thing Mrs. Chong gave her warning. When the train stopped and the doors opened, Sue was almost trampled by the passengers rushing out. At times like these, she regretted not being heavier, so she would be harder to knock over.

Sue stumbled out of the train and followed the Chongs through the exit gate. They walked across a railway overpass, down some iron steps, and through narrow streets. There were small shops on both sides of the street, but Sue was too tired to look closely at them. Anyway, sweat stung her eyes and prevented her from seeing clearly. The heat and humidity began to hit her really hard.

"Here we are," said Mr. Chong's voice.

Sue blinked the sweat from her eyes and looked up. They were stopped in front of a wooden gate. Mr. Chong lifted the small metal loop holding the two doors of the gate together and pushed it open. Facing them was a low wooden house. Even Sue could tell that this was not the home of a wealthy family. She should have realized it sooner, since the Chongs did not own a car, and they could not afford to call a taxi from the station to their house.

Perhaps Mr. Chong read Sue's thoughts. "Please excuse our poor house," he said. "I hope you won't find it too uncomfortable."

"I'm lucky to be staying with a family as musical as yours," said Sue, and she meant it wholeheartedly.

Sue immediately took her shoes off upon entering the house. Mrs. Chong nodded her approval and brought Sue a pair of slippers. "You have been to Japan before?"

"No," said Sue. "My boyfriend told me about taking off my shoes inside the house."

Mrs. Chong looked relieved. "Good! Then he also told you about Japanese-style toilets and baths?"

Uh-oh. They have different toilets? "Uh . . . I'm afraid not."

"All right," said Mrs. Chong with a sigh. "I'd better show you, after we bring your things to your room."

Sue followed her hostess to a tiny, neat room. A desk and chair stood on one side of the room, while most of the remaining area was taken up by a thin mattress spread out on the floor.

"This is our daughter's room, but she is away this summer to stay with friends," explained Mrs. Chong. "I've unfolded the futon for you since I know you must be tired and will want to rest. You can fold it up again to-morrow morning." She pulled back a sliding door and revealed a shallow closet with shelves. "You can put away the futon here, and also your suitcase."

After Sue deposited her things, she followed Mrs. Chong down the hall and around a corner. "Here is the toilet," said her hostess, sliding back a small door. "Have you ever used a pit toilet before?"

Sue gulped and shook her head. *Pit toilet. That sounds awful.* "But I've heard about them. I know that they're used a lot in China."

"That's right," said Mrs. Chong. "They're also common in Turkey, Russia, and some other countries."

Sue looked down at the toilet, which was essentially a hole in the floor. It consisted of a long, narrow porcelain basin with a raised edge at one end and a big drainage hole. Judging from the lever at one end, Sue knew that it was at least a flush toilet. She guessed that the user would be squatting over the basin, facing the raised edge. "I'll manage, I think," she said shakily. She was too exhausted to even think about it.

"You'll want to take a bath, too," said Mrs. Chong. She led Sue down the hall and into a small corner room. The floor consisted of wooden slats, placed some distance apart for drainage. Standing in a corner was a deep wooden box, about three feet square. "There's our bathtub," said Mrs. Chong.

The wooden tub was set on a metal box that looked like a gas stove, and was half filled with hot water. Sue didn't see any faucets for cold water. She stared at the steam curling up and fought down her panic. Trying to sound casual, she asked, "After bathing, how do I empty the tub and refill it for other people?"

"You don't have to," said Mrs. Chong. "You soap and rinse yourself outside, and then step into the tub for a nice, hot soak. Since you're clean when you step into the tub, we can all use the same water."

Ugh. And a hot bath would feel so good right now. "I think I'll just wash and rinse myself outside the tub," said Sue. Nothing on earth would persuade her to climb into that steaming box.

Mrs. Chong chuckled. "We've had guests from America before. They always seem to want to avoid that tub."

Sue smiled. At least she wasn't insulting her host.

After that, Mrs. Chong led Sue back to her room and told her she would give her some time to freshen up. Sue had thought that she would drop from tiredness, but after washing and changing into fresh clothes, she felt clean, vigorous, and very hungry.

Following her nose, she arrived in a small room that had a dining table on one side and a stove on the other. "My husband has gone back to work," Mrs. Chong told Sue. "We run a convenience store that stays open late. It's just around the corner." She began putting dishes of food on the table. "Come and eat. Did you have a good wash?"

"Yes, thank you," said Sue. "But I didn't climb into the box—I mean tub."

Mrs. Chong laughed. "I know. After the huge bathtubs in America, our tub here must look like a box. In fact, everything must seem small to you."

It was true. Compared with the rooms of Sue's house back home, all the rooms in the Chong residence felt tiny. The dining table here was the size of a coffee table, and the refrigerator in the corner of the kitchen didn't look much bigger than a picnic ice chest. "I guess we're spoiled in America, living in a huge country with so much space."

Some of the food that Mrs. Chong set out looked and smelled like the stir-fried dishes Sue's mother made. In the eating utensils, Sue found differences from both the Chinese and Japanese varieties. The chopsticks were metal, as was the soup spoon.

The food was delicious, and Sue began to devour everything Mrs. Chong put before her. "I didn't really expect to eat this well," Sue told her hostess. "I like eating some kinds of Japanese food, like tempura, and I don't mind sushi. But after a while, I get tired of things made with cold, sour rice."

Mrs. Chong looked pleased. "I'm glad you like my cooking. I hope it makes up for our toilet and bath facilities."

Sue blushed. She hadn't realized that her discomfort had been so obvious. "I'm sorry to make so much trouble for you."

"It's a pleasure to have you," said Mrs. Chong. "As I said, talking with you brings back happy memories of my years in America."

"Did some of the other host families spend time in America, too?" asked Sue.

"Maybe some of them did," said Mrs. Chong, "but I'm not sure. I don't know the other parents very well. Not many of them live around here, you see."

Something in the way she spoke made Sue suspect that there was another reason that the Chongs were not close friends with the other parents. Mrs. Chong must have read Sue's thoughts. "When you go to the Kasei School tomorrow, you'll discover that our family is different from the others," she began. "For one thing, their homes are more luxurious than ours, and more modern. Most have Western-style toilets, not a hole in the floor. Their bathtubs are made of fiberglass, and the hot water comes from taps. Our house is in an old-fashioned part of town, and the facilities date back to the nineteenth century."

"I'm surprised there are old houses left in Tokyo,"

said Sue. She had read about the Second World War, so she knew that most of the houses in Tokyo had been destroyed by American firebombing.

"It's true that very few old houses are left," said Mrs. Chong. "In fact, much of Tokyo had already been destroyed by the Kanto earthquake of 1923 and the fire that followed. The only part of this house from the old days is the bathroom. It survived both the quake and the bombing. It probably dates back to feudal times!"

Sue and her hostess both laughed. But Sue was puzzled. "It must be expensive to send your daughter to the Toho School," she remarked. As soon as she said it, she realized that she had been tactless.

Mrs. Chong's lips twisted. "The school *is* expensive, but we can afford the tuition. I make good money giving music lessons."

Sue was still puzzled, and Mrs. Chong went on to explain. "We are not well acquainted with the other parents at Kasei, but it's not just because we are less wealthy than they are. It's because we're Koreans."

Sue was shocked. She couldn't help thinking of her own family's relations with their neighbors.

Again, Mrs. Chong seemed to guess Sue's thoughts. "You don't suffer discrimination in America because you're Asian?"

"Maybe a little," said Sue, trying to be completely honest. "When I started at my new school, which has mostly white students, the other kids sort of stared at me like I was something weird. But once they got used to me, they forgot I was different."

"They forgot you're not a 'real' American," murmured Mrs. Chong.

"It used to be a lot worse, though," Sue admitted. "My parents tell me that in the old days, white people jeered at the Chinese by shouting 'Ching, Ching, China-man!' But it's much better than it used to be, and our schools have programs that promote multiculturalism."

"Even black people are accepted these days?" asked Mrs. Chong. She looked doubtful. "When I went to school in America, there was still quite a bit of discrimination against blacks. I heard that even today the police stop black drivers much more often than they do white drivers."

"Well, unfortunately, that's true," admitted Sue. "There's still a lot of racial tension in America. I think it goes back to slavery. It's a hard thing to overcome."

Somehow that comment brought a sudden change in the air. Mrs. Chong's face hardened.

"I'm sorry," said Sue. "Did I say something wrong?"

"Do you know the history of the Koreans in Japan?" asked Mrs. Chong.

Sue shook her head. She knew that Korea had once been invaded by Japan, but she didn't know the details. She knew that China had invaded Korea, as well, although that had happened a lot earlier.

Mrs. Chong took a deep breath. "The Japanese first invaded Korea in the sixteenth century, but they didn't stay. Then they invaded again at the beginning of the twentieth century, and in 1910, Korea became a Japanese colony."

Sue knew that parts of China had been occupied by various foreigners. But to have your whole country made into a colony must be much worse. Sue was sorry she had mentioned the subject, but there was no stopping Mrs. Chong now.

"During the 1940s, many Koreans were brought to Japan as forced labor," continued Mrs. Chong. "They had to do the lowest kind of menial work. My grandparents, as well as my husband's, were among those who were brought here."

Sue swallowed. "What happened after the war? After Japan was defeated in 1945, all the Koreans must have been free to go home."

Mrs. Chong smiled bitterly. "Some Koreans did go home. Others, like my grandparents, decided to stay in Japan until things became more stable in Korea. You see, there were various forces trying to gain control of the peninsula. Do you know anything about the Korean War?"

Sue nodded. She had read up on the war, and she also learned some things from watching programs like *M*A*S*H*. Her parents had discussed the Korean War, since China—Communist China—had been fighting on the side of North Korea.

"My grandparents' family were from North Korea," continued Mrs. Chong. "They didn't like what was happening there, and they made the decision to stay in Japan."

"Then you're the third generation to be living here," said Sue. She compared Mrs. Chong's case with her own: Sue's grandparents had moved to America when her mother was a young girl, and Sue had been born in the States. She felt like an American. "So do you feel completely Japanese?" she asked her hostess.

Again Mrs. Chong's lips twisted. "We are not allowed to feel completely Japanese. Many Koreans aren't even citizens."

"But . . . but . . . you were born here!" cried Sue. She knew that even babies born to illegal immigrants who had sneaked across the border from Mexico were U.S. citizens.

"That doesn't mean we're automatically citizens," said Mrs. Chong. "Koreans living in Japan have to apply for citizenship, and it is granted only after a thorough investigation of the applicant's background. Until we obtain citizenship, we have no civil rights."

Sue was shocked. "In America, people are sometimes discriminated against because of the way they look—their skin color, shape of their noses, and things. But you look just like a Japanese! How can they discriminate against you if they can't even tell you apart?"

Mrs. Chong sat silent for a minute. Then she said, "Take the Jews in Nazi Germany. Some of them looked completely Aryan, with blond hair and blue eyes. Yet they were rounded up and sent to concentration camps. So it's not how you look or act but who your ancestors are that's important."

Sue picked the last few grains of rice from her bowl and thought over Mrs. Chong's words. "I guess in America people don't make such a big deal about your ancestors," she said finally. "Maybe it's because everybody's an immigrant, or descended from immigrants."

"Exactly!" said Mrs. Chong. "You asked how people can discriminate against somebody who doesn't look different from them. Have you heard about the Burakumin?"

When Sue shook her head, Mrs. Chong explained. "The Burakumin are called the untouchables of Japan. Although they are completely identical to other Japanese racially, they've been discriminated against for centuries."

"You mean like the untouchables in India?" asked Sue. Her friend Nareen, who had gone to Sue's old school, was from India, and she had told her that there were different castes, or classes of Indian society. What caste you belonged to depended on who your ancestors were. The untouchables were the lowest caste, although you couldn't tell by just looking at them.

Mrs. Chong nodded. "That's a very good comparison! The Burakumin in Japan don't look different, and some have tried to pass as regular Japanese."

Sue had thought the caste system in India was strange, but this Japanese untouchable class was just as weird. "What started the discrimination against the Burakumin in the first place?" she asked.

"I'm not sure," said Mrs. Chong. "I've heard it may be due to their occupation. Hundreds of years ago, certain people were hired to dispose of corpses, kill animals— do work connected with slaughtering. Many of these people became leather workers, which was considered a disgusting occupation because it involved killing animals and tanning their skins."

Sue thought of some friends who were vegetarians. "I

know people who refuse to eat food from animals. But they don't consider us meat eaters untouchables."

"Killing animals was against Buddhist principles," explained Mrs. Chong. "So a leather worker tainted not only himself, but also his family and all his descendants."

"But at least these untouchables have civil rights, don't they?" asked Sue. "So how can the rest of the Japanese discriminate against them, especially if you can't tell them apart?"

"Parents don't want their children to marry the Burakumin," said Mrs. Chong. "When young people get engaged, sometimes their parents hire a detective to look into the family of the fiancé or fiancée, to make sure there are no skeletons in the closet, like a relative who is an untouchable."

Sue was shocked. She tried to imagine Grandma Mei hiring a detective to see if Andy's family was Japanese. It boggled her mind. "There's this girl in the orchestra called Ginny," she said. "She notices only how people look, so she lumps Chinese, Japanese, and Koreans together because we all have the same hair and eyes and skin. I bet she'd be *really* confused by the Burakumin!"

"While you're here, you may discover that some Japanese discriminate against the Chinese, especially those who came to this country looking for work," Mrs. Chong warned. She looked curiously at Sue. "You Chinese have also suffered a lot from the Japanese invasion. Don't you resent them for what they did to your country?"

Sue was startled to hear the phrase "you Chinese"

used in connection with herself, and to hear China called "your country." At school, the teachers and other kids referred to her as a Chinese American. "I don't know much about the invasion," she muttered. "But my grandmother was in China at the time, and she saw some horrible things."

"But what about *you*?" asked Mrs. Chong. "How do *you* feel, now that you're actually in enemy country?"

Enemy country? Maybe that's how Grandma Mei thinks of Japan, but not me. Sue remembered her father's story about Professor Hasegawa. "Not all the Japanese people supported the invasion. Some of them openly opposed what the government did, and they paid a price for it." She looked curiously at Mrs. Chong. She seemed so bitter, so very angry at her country. Sue knew that America wasn't perfect, but she couldn't imagine feeling as fed up as Mrs. Chong seemed to be. "You've lived in Japan all your life. Haven't you met anybody who's been nice to you?"

Mrs. Chong's mouth dropped open. Finally she said, "You're right, of course. Once I start, I can think of a great number of Japanese who have been kind to us: the parents of some of my students, the farmer who supplies my husband with fresh vegetables, some of the teachers at the Kasei School . . ." She stared at Sue. "You're a remarkable young lady. I don't often meet teenagers with such a generous heart."

Sue was touched. Some girls might prefer to be called beautiful or sexy, but this compliment from her hostess was the nicest she could imagine.

Mrs. Chong got up, put the dirty dishes in the sink, and began to run water over them. "Let me help you," said Sue. "I can dry."

"No, you'd better lie down and rest," said her hostess. "You must be exhausted by your trip."

Suddenly Sue realized Mrs. Chong was right. She was totally exhausted.

"Tomorrow the Kasei School has planned an outing for your orchestra," said Mrs. Chong. Her voice already seemed to come from a great distance.

As Sue stumbled toward her room, she wondered how the rest of the Lakeview kids were doing with their hosts. What was Andy's host family like?

andy woke up at three in the morning Tokyo time and couldn't get back to sleep. After tossing and turning for a while, he decided to try his old trick: he picked the most boring piece of music he knew and visualized the score. By the time he reached the second page of the score, he was asleep again. The next time he opened his eyes, his watch said five-thirty in the morning. At home he wouldn't think of getting up at this hour, but considering the time difference, he knew he wouldn't be able to sleep again. In fact, he felt well rested and raring to go.

The question was, go where? Very quietly, Andy got dressed and gently slid his door open. He walked down the hall in his bare feet, afraid that his slippers would make a *slish slish* sound and disturb the others.

When he reached the front entrance, he took his shoes from the shelf and slipped them on, stepped down to ground level, quietly turned the key, and slid the front door open. Then he stepped outside into the morning air.

It was wonderful. Taking a deep breath of the cool air, Andy walked across the stepping-stones and went around the house to the back garden, which he hadn't seen yet. It was much bigger than the front garden and was immaculately groomed in the Zen style.

In spite of his father's attempts to teach him, Andy had never learned to like this dry, bare kind of Japanese garden. To him, there had never been anything special about the swirls of sand and few lonely pieces of rock. But now, in the peaceful morning light, there was something magical about it.

He heard a door being opened and found Mr. Sato standing on the wooden veranda overlooking the garden.

"Ohayo gozaimasu," said Andy. It meant good morning, and was one of the phrases he had practiced.

Mr. Sato was still wearing a cotton kimono. He stepped down from the veranda and pushed his feet into a pair of wooden clogs. "Did you sleep well?" he asked.

"Very well," said Andy, and decided that a tiny bow would be appropriate. *When in doubt, always bow.* "This garden is great!" he said.

His enthusiasm was genuine, and Mr. Sato beamed with pleasure. "You like? Even without colorful flowers?"

"It's in the Zen style, isn't it?" said Andy. "My father tried to teach me to appreciate it."

Mr. Sato beamed even more, and Andy could feel his approval rating soar. He hoped he could keep it up.

"It is early, but in summer we like to get up early to enjoy cool air," said Mr. Sato. "You would like breakfast, yes?"

Andy's father had warned him that a traditional Japanese breakfast involved hot rice, bean paste soup, broiled fish, pickles, and sometimes a raw egg on top of the rice. He was so hungry that all of that actually sounded good to him. "Just watch me!"

Mr. Sato chuckled and told Andy to follow him inside. He stepped out of his clogs, while Andy removed his shoes. They stepped up to the veranda, and Mr. Sato pushed open a pair of latticed doors covered with white paper. Andy found himself in a room furnished in the traditional Japanese style. The floor was covered by reed tatami mats, and there were no chairs, only a low table with some big flat cushions around it for seating. One side of the room had some shelves and a flower arrangement. Hanging on the wall behind the flowers was an ink painting.

Andy thought the picture looked like the kind Mrs. Hua painted. "This is in the literati style, isn't it?" he asked.

This time he hit the jackpot. "You know the style?" cried Mr. Sato, sounding astonished.

Andy nodded. "My father likes this kind of painting." He was sure that by now he must have earned enough points to tide him over for the rest of the visit. He looked around the room and saw a shelf with two samurai swords resting on a rack.

Mr. Sato noticed Andy's glance. "The swords belonged to my ancestors. Normally, I would hand them down to my son. But I have only a daughter, Haruko." He added after a moment, "Of course, we could adopt a boy."

Andy didn't know what to say to that, so he just nodded. For the first time he felt a little sorry for Haruko. Then he remembered the way she'd scowled at him and decided his sympathy was wasted.

The door behind him opened and Mrs. Sato poked her head in. "Oh, you are awake. Shall we have breakfast?"

Putting his shoes away in the cupboard, Andy went into the same room where he had eaten supper. The table was set for a breakfast that looked Western.

Behind him, the door slid open, and the elder Mr. Sato came in, supported by Haruko. The old man was not crippled, but he walked with difficulty, perhaps from arthritis. Haruko carefully guided her grandfather to his chair and smiled down at him. It was a surprisingly tender smile. Haruko then seated herself.

At a gesture from his hostess, Andy sat in the same seat he had had the night before. In front of him was a plate with two slices of toast, the bread almost an inch thick. There was also an egg cup with a boiled egg that was still warm, and an empty teacup and saucer. Although he usually had a big bowl of cereal and a glass of orange juice for breakfast, Andy was more than happy to dive in.

Mrs. Sato passed him some butter and a little bowl of

strawberry jam. *"Kocha?"* she asked. Seeing that he was puzzled, she explained, "Kocha is black tea."

At home Andy seldom drank black tea, though his parents occasionally drank green tea. "Sure," replied Andy, and held out his teacup. "So you eat a Western breakfast with toast and everything," he said.

"You were expecting us to eat like peasants in the countryside, maybe?" demanded Haruko. "After breakfast, I suppose you will join us in the fields to transplant rice seedlings?"

Back to the old Haruko.

"Haruko!" Mrs. Sato protested weakly.

Andy was determined to keep his temper. "I'm just going by what my father tells me. He loves to talk about staying at traditional inns where he was served a raw egg on top of hot rice for breakfast. So I guess that was what I was expecting."

"That's what I like, too," said Mr. Sato. "It seems that Andy's father and I have the same tastes in gardens and paintings, as well."

Haruko scowled. Mrs. Sato hurriedly poured some tea for her daughter and put two slices of bread in the toaster.

Andy still couldn't figure out why Haruko was so unfriendly to him. The way she behaved toward her grandfather showed that she did have a softer side. He resolved that before he went back to America, he would make Haruko respect him—not necessarily like, just respect.

* * *

The Lakeview kids had been instructed to gather in front of the Kasei School. Andy and Haruko were driven to the school by Mr. Sato. The narrow streets were jammed with morning traffic, so progress was very slow, and they were among the last to arrive.

Andy saw that Sue was already there. When she saw him, she broke into the shy smile he loved. He had to fight down an urge to rush over and grab her and kiss her hard. In Japan, doing something like that in public would be totally shocking. Even if they were back in America, people like their parents would disapprove.

Sue must have seen something in his eyes, because her face turned red. She cleared her throat. "How did it go with your host family?" she asked when Andy made his way over to her.

"Pretty good," he said. "Let me introduce . . ." He looked around for Haruko and found that she was no longer with him. He turned back to Sue. "Never mind. What's your host family like?"

"I'm staying with the Chongs," said Sue. "They seem nice. They're Korean, not Japanese."

"You mean Korean Korean, Korean Japanese, or Korean American?" asked Andy.

Sue grimaced. "The Chongs have been in Japan for three generations, but they're still not citizens. So that makes them Korean Korean, I guess."

"So do they have one of their kids here at the Kasei School?" asked Andy.

Sue shook her head. "Their daughter went to school

here, and she was in the orchestra when it toured the States last year. But she's graduated, and she's now going to a music academy."

Sue began to describe the discrimination experienced by the Chongs. Andy was shocked when he heard that most of the Kasei parents didn't mix with the Chongs because they were Korean. He thought about the rude way Haruko treated him. If she was like that with him, he could only imagine what she would be like with the Chongs.

"I don't think the Chongs are poor," added Sue. "They run a convenience store, and Mrs. Chong teaches music. They can send their daughter to the Toho School of Music, which is pretty expensive."

"Weird," said Andy. "Every once in a while, someone will say something offensive to me back home. But I've definitely never felt that kind of discrimination. My grandfather said when he first moved to America, he was called names and stuff. But it doesn't seem that bad in America anymore."

"Mrs. Chong also told me there's prejudice against the Chinese here," said Sue. "It's because so many Chinese came over from mainland China to look for work. I guess some of the younger people got into trouble and formed gangs, so many Japanese think that all Chinese are hoodlums. I wonder if that's why they put me with a Korean family, because both Koreans and Chinese are inferior people."

Andy was shocked. "You really think they believe that? Just tell them what my mom told me: the Japanese were illiterate until they learned reading and writing from the Chinese!"

Before Sue could say more, Andy heard a voice behind him. "Hi, lovebirds!" said Mia. "Hey, Andy, this girl here says you're staying with her family."

Mia was standing with Haruko, who was now smiling happily. "She says she's Harko . . . Harpo . . ." Mia stumbled over the name and gave up.

"This is Sato Haruko," said Andy. "Her parents have a gorgeous house, and their garden is like something you'd see in a magazine."

Ginny and Nathan joined them, and Andy saw that Haruko's eyes brightened as more of the Lakeview kids came up to talk. The players began to compare their experiences. Laurie was staying with a family whose daughter had stayed with Laurie's family when she visited Seattle the year before. Nathan was staying with the family of the trumpet player who had been his guest.

Andy envied Laurie, Nathan, and others who were reunited with the Japanese kids they knew. He, on the other hand, was stuck with Haruko, who stared at him coldly, when she bothered to look at him at all. Maybe Haruko was just stuck-up. Andy got the impression that the Satos were among the wealthier parents at the Kasei School. Also, they were from a samurai family.

"I've been learning to eat on the floor," Nathan was saying. Some of the other kids laughed, and he explained. "This family I'm staying with, they have normal kinds of furniture in most of the rooms, but there's one room in the Japanese style. The floor is covered by tatami mats, and you sit on cushions."

"The Satos have that, too," said Andy. He turned to Haruko. "I saw the Japanese-style room in your house."

Haruko did not look pleased at this reminder. She gave a curt nod and turned away.

"So how do you feel after sitting on the floor all through dinner?" Nathan asked Andy. "Maybe you're used to it, being Japanese and all. But by the end of the meal, I felt like a million ants were crawling up my legs. When I tried to stand up afterwards, my legs were so numb that I almost fell over. Thank God we ate breakfast in the kitchen this morning!"

"They were giving you a special welcome," Andy explained. "Serving dinner in the Japanese room takes more work. I just ate at a regular table."

Then, realizing that his remark might be interpreted to mean that Haruko's family had been less welcoming, Andy glanced quickly at her. But she had her back to him and was busy talking to Mia. *I'm going to make Haruko look at me with respect, if it's the last thing I do.*

The school bell rang, and the Japanese kids went off to their classes. "Should we just wait here? Do you know what we're supposed to be doing this morning?" Andy asked Sue.

"Mrs. Chong said something about a field trip they've planned for us," said Sue.

Mr. Baxter came up and called the players together. "The principal of the Kasei School said that you're probably all suffering jet lag. So instead of rehearsals today, he's arranged to have us take the day off for some sightseeing. We'll start work tomorrow."

Andy was relieved. His stomach had already begun

to flutter at the thought of playing his solo. Now he had a reprieve—at least for the day.

"They're taking us to a town called Kamakura, where we'll be spending the day," Mr. Baxter went on. "It's a couple of hours by bus from Tokyo."

Sue looked excited as they waited for the bus. "Kamakura was the capital of the first shogun, who was the leader of the samurai and the ruler of Japan during the middle ages," she said.

"How come you know so much about the shogun and samurai and things?" Mia asked Sue.

"She likes stuff about warfare," said Andy.

"My mom took me and my sister to all those antiwar demonstrations," said Sue. "So I wanted to understand why some men would kill people and destroy cities and villages, even men like knights and samurai, who talked a lot about honor."

"Did I hear someone mention samurai?" said Nathan, coming over. "I love stories about the samurai. They were so honorable, so powerful, you know?"

"The samurai weren't always on top," said Andy. He felt a certain satisfaction in saying this. His father's family had originally been farmers, not samurai. "Earlier, the court nobles were at the top, and the samurai were simply attendants for their betters. In fact, the word 'samurai' means attendant."

"If the shogun was just the head attendant, how did he become the ruler of Japan, then?" asked Nathan.

Andy didn't know the answer, and neither did Sue. Their bus arrived, and after they piled in and seated themselves, a woman with a mike got up in the front of the bus and introduced herself as their guide for the day.

"Let us start with a brief history of Kamakura," she began. "In the eleventh century, the emperor became weak and the warrior samurai class rose in power. One leading warrior family, the Minamotos, defeated all their rivals . . ."

Andy saw that Sue was listening eagerly to the guide's words. He tried hard to follow what the guide was saying, but her voice was soft and soothing, like a lullaby. . . .

The bus made a sudden turn and Andy's eyes popped open. He realized that he must have been dozing. The guide was now talking about some famous Zen Buddhist temples.

Andy saw that even Sue had fallen asleep. Her interest in military history couldn't keep her awake. He smiled as he watched her silky curtain of hair fluff up and down with her soft breathing. He looked around and found his fellow players all asleep. Even Mr. Baxter was slumped in his seat, dead to the world.

Unfazed, the guide talked on. Andy struggled very hard to keep his eyes open, but it was a losing battle. The last words he heard from the guide were ". . . other Buddhist sects . . . the great bronze statue of Buddha . . ."

"We have arrived," said the voice of the guide. Andy opened his eyes and discovered that the bus was stopped and the guide was standing by the open door. "Please watch your step when going down," she said with a faint smile.

Once the students were outside, the fresh air revived them. Andy was glad to find Kamakura cooler than Tokyo. Being near the sea also made the air breezier. "We start our visit with the Hachiman Shrine," the guide told them.

The shrine consisted of a complex of buildings painted in brilliant orange. The guide stopped in front of a raised open-air stage and told the story of a famous performance.

"Although the shogun Yoritomo became the most powerful man in Japan, he was still jealous of his younger brother, Yoshitsune, who was a brilliant soldier. Yoritomo not only hounded his brother to death, but forced his brother's mistress, a beautiful lady called Shizuka, to dance for him on this very platform."

"Can you believe that?" Sue said indignantly. "And those samurai had the nerve to talk about their code of honor!"

Startled, the guide turned to look at Sue, and Andy had to turn away to hide his grin. Most people noticed only Sue's shy exterior, and were startled by her flashes of spirit.

The guide cleared her throat and went on. "Yoritomo's family did not enjoy their power for long. When he died, he left only two young sons, and both of them suffered untimely deaths."

They began to climb a steep flight of stone steps. The guide pointed at an immense ginkgo tree by the side of the steps. "Yoritomo's second son, Sanetomo, was killed right here. His assassin hid behind this tree and ambushed him."

Nathan shook his head. "That's awesome! See, that's why I love stories about the samurai. Nonstop action. Wouldn't that make a great movie, like with Tom Cruise and . . ."

The guide heard him. "There have been countless movies and plays about these incidents already."

They walked past a stand selling little wooden plaques with a picture of a horse painted on one side. "You buy one of these and write a wish on the blank side," the guide told them. She pointed at a frame where a lot of the wooden plaques were hung, with writing on one side. "Most of the wishes have to do with success in business, or passing entrance examinations and getting admitted to a good college."

Andy looked at the plaques. Almost all of them were in Japanese, but there were a few in English, and even one in French. Some of the Lakeview kids thought it would be fun to make wishes, and they went over to a booth selling the plaques.

A horn player, who was a junior, said he hoped he would do well on his college board exams next year. Ginny had fought with her boyfriend just before leaving for Japan and was wondering what he was doing back home. "I want to make sure he's behaving," she said, writing quickly on her wooden plaque.

Andy heard Mia saying to Sue, "Guess you and Andy don't need to make wishes about each other."

Sue blushed, and Andy had to smile. Then he had an idea. He bought one of the plaques and wrote on the back, "I wish Haruko would stop looking at me like I'm such a loser."

"What are you wishing for?" Sue's voice said behind him.

Andy jumped. "Nothing much. I just wished that Haruko would stop being a jerk to me."

Sue looked surprised, and a little bit hurt. "Why do you care so much?" she asked sharply.

Suddenly Andy felt embarrassed. *Does she think it's weird that Haruko bugs me? Is she jealous?* "Look, never mind. It's not important." He tossed the plaque into a nearby trash can.

After leaving the shrine, the guide told them it was time for lunch. *Bento,* or lunch boxes, had been prepared for them while they were touring the shrine. The guide led them to an area with benches and small tables shaded by tall trees. They each picked up a box, as well as a small plastic bottle that turned out to contain lukewarm green tea.

Andy had eaten bento boxes back home in Seattle, where they were sold in many supermarkets. They usually contained pieces of sushi and slices of ginger. The bento box he opened now was quite different. It had a pile of white rice, a piece of broiled salmon, a slice of red and white fish paste shaped like a flower, a piece of boiled squash, yellow pickled radish, and items that even he didn't recognize.

Several of the kids broke apart their wooden chopsticks but hesitated to start eating. Andy knew that most of them had learned to use chopsticks while preparing for the trip, but some of them were not sure how they felt about the strange food.

"What's this?" asked Nathan, pointing at a small sausage. "It looks like a hot dog."

Andy took a bite of his sausage. "It *is* a hot dog."

Hunger won out, and soon everyone was digging in. "I can't believe how good that was!" said Ginny. "And I don't even like fish!"

The program for the afternoon included visits to some Buddhist temples. Andy knew the difference between a Shinto shrine and a Buddhist temple, but the guide had to explain to the others. "Shinto is the state religion of Japan. The Hachiman Shrine we just visited is Shinto. Buddhism, on the other hand, is a religion imported from India by way of China."

The guide took them to a Zen temple first. "Kamakura is famous for its five great Zen Buddhist temples. The Zen sect is particularly favored by the samurai class. We can say that Zen Buddhism began its rise here."

Sue suddenly spoke up. "Zen Buddhism actually began at the Shaolin Temple in China. That temple is also famous for being the home of the monks who developed the kung fu style of fighting."

Surprised, the guide turned again to stare at Sue. Andy grinned at Sue and gave a thumbs-up sign.

The Zen temple they visited was Kencho-ji, which stood under a hill with ancient juniper trees. There was such a feeling of peace that Andy found it hard to believe that Zen was the religion of the samurai class and the warrior monks of Shaolin Temple.

Even Ginny, usually the loudest of the students, fell silent as the guide told them all to stop and listen. They heard the liquid sound of a birdcall. "The bird is called an *uguisu,* or Japanese nightingale," said the guide.

The melodious birdcall made Andy think of Mozart's *Magic Flute.* He was totally entranced by the call of the nightingale, the fragrance of the juniper trees, and the serenity of the temple. When the guide told them it was time to go, Andy was the last one to pass through the temple gate.

Their next visit was to the Great Buddha. Andy had seen photos of the bronze statue, but he was still overwhelmed by the real thing. The half-closed eyes and the hands resting on the lap gave the figure a feeling of total calm and repose.

On their way back to the bus depot, the guide allowed the kids a few minutes to browse along a shopping street, which was lined on both sides with stalls containing colorful merchandise. "Wow! Look at this scarf!" cried Ginny. A couple of the other girls also started picking up things: a tiny doll, a necklace, a miniature model of a shrine gate . . .

Andy bought some postcards, while Sue looked over some of the things in one of the stalls. "I want to get something special for my grandmother."

"Why your grandmother?" asked Andy. "What about the rest of the family?"

"Grandma was very upset at the airport," Sue said softly. "I feel I really let her down."

Andy remembered the old woman's fury when she found out his family was Japanese. "Are you going to let your grandmother rule your life?" he demanded.

Sue shook her head. "No, I'm not!"

That wasn't good enough for Andy. "Sue, you're not going to let your grandmother break us up, are you?"

"Of course not!" Sue said quickly. "But I hurt her feelings, and I want to make it up to her."

Andy wasn't completely satisfied, but there was nothing he could do. *I've got to think of some way to take care of Grandma.*

Sue went over to look at some lacquerware in one of the stalls. "Our guide said Kamakura is famous for its lacquer," she told Andy. "Maybe I can buy a dish or a bowl for Grandma."

Sue picked up a bowl whose outside was rough, unpainted wood, and whose inside was lacquered in bright orange. "Um . . . I like this," she murmured, and turned it over to look at the price tag. She yelped and hurriedly put it down again.

"Let's wait until we get back to Tokyo," Andy told her. Anyway, it was time to leave, and the guide was calling people over to the bus.

"My dad will probably want a full report on the outing," said Andy as the bus brought them back to Tokyo. The thought depressed him. He knew his father would want to hear how impressed he was, how at home he felt in this place he had never been to before. But Andy felt as much like an outsider here as his classmates.

"You can tell him about seeing the Great Buddha and the Zen temples, and the stage where that lady was forced to dance," suggested Sue.

"Yeah, but those are the things other tourists talk about," said Andy. "I want to tell him about some special experience I had, some connection I felt to the place." Then he smiled. "I know what. I'm going to tell him about the nightingale!"

On Friday, the day after their excursion to Kamakura, the Lakeview orchestra went to the Kasei School for their first rehearsal.

Again, Mr. Sato drove Andy and Haruko to the school. Andy felt well rested, and breakfast with the Sato family went more smoothly now that he was familiar with the routine. He made fewer mistakes, and when he asked for the jam in the correct Japanese, *"Chotto, jamu o kochirai,"* he saw approval in the eyes of the older Mr. Sato. At this rate, they might even begin to treat him like family. But the women, Mrs. Sato and especially Haruko, still looked at him with disapproval.

Haruko and other Japanese students went off to their classes while the Lakeview kids waited for Mr. Baxter. He showed up a few minutes later, and Andy thought the conductor looked slightly tense. His shoulders were hunched, and he chewed his lips for a few seconds before addressing the players. *So I'm not the only one suffering from stage fright.*

Mr. Baxter took a deep breath. "Okay, people, the principal tells me that the auditorium is now open. Let's go in. We've got some rehearsing to do."

It was one of the worst rehearsals Andy had ever played in. The orchestra was still not completely recovered from jet lag. Andy, like other string players, found that his fiddle had to be drastically retuned. Maybe it was the change in altitude from the flight, or the high humidity in Tokyo. The bassoon player complained that his reeds were sulking, and he played an ugly *blaht* to prove it.

Andy became even more nervous when Laurie told him that the conductor of the Kasei orchestra was in the auditorium listening to them. When they broke for lunch, the conductor came up to talk to Mr. Baxter, and Andy heard some of the exchange.

"You'll have to excuse us," Mr. Baxter was saying. "The players haven't gotten over their jet lag yet. And I'm not doing much better."

"Please don't worry," said the Kasei conductor. "Our orchestra had a hard time, too, when we first arrived in America. You'll be fine in a couple of days."

The Lakeview players ate in the lunchroom with the

Kasei students. The lunchroom had narrower tables than the ones at Lakeview, and it was a lot more crowded. Space was simply more limited. That was the impression Andy had of the school building as well. Otherwise, things didn't look all that different.

In the lunchroom, some of the Lakeview players went to sit with students from their host families. Andy looked around for Haruko and found her already at a table with Mia and Ginny. Andy and Sue went over to join them. Squeezing himself into the space on the bench, Andy thought that it was almost like being back in the Lakeview lunchroom.

A Japanese student sat down next to Andy. He spoke a little English, and he and Andy began to compare school schedules. "You already on vacation," the Japanese boy said enviously. "Our summer vacation starts at beginning of August, and it lasts only one month."

"No kidding!" said Andy. *I guess American students are pretty lucky.* "What are you planning to do on your vacation?"

The Japanese boy made a face. "Before I enjoy vacation, I have science project to do."

Andy was puzzled. "Then who grades your homework? Your teacher for this year, or your teacher for next year?"

The Japanese boy explained that the new school year in Japan didn't start in September. "I still have same teacher after summer vacation. I don't go up to next grade until April first."

It became too strenuous for the Japanese boy to

continue the English conversation. He exchanged a few polite phrases with Andy and went back to talking in Japanese to his friends on the other side.

With Haruko busy talking to Mia and the Japanese student talking to his friends, Andy and Sue found they had some privacy. It was almost like being at Hero's again, except that the food was different. Instead of a sandwich, Andy had a little plastic bento box provided by Mrs. Sato. It contained a simpler version of the bento he had eaten in Kamakura. "What have you got for lunch?" he asked Sue.

Sue showed him a plastic box containing a slice of meat with some vegetables and potatoes. "It comes from Mr. Chong's convenience store," she said.

Just then, Haruko broke out laughing as she chatted with some of the Lakeview students. The sound of her laughter grated on Andy. "I don't think Haruko has ever laughed at anything I've said," Andy said to Sue. "What's so funny about Mia and Ginny?"

Sue frowned. "I don't get why she bothers you so much. She's not a nice person. Get over it."

"Yeah, but then she's nice to Mia and Ginny. I don't understand it," said Andy.

"She's the one you wanted to write about on that wooden plaque in the Kamakura shrine, right?" asked Sue.

Andy nodded a little defensively. "Yeah, well, I just got tired of being sneered at all the time."

"But she seems nice enough now," said Sue.

Andy sighed. Nobody understood how weird

Haruko was with him. She was sweet and friendly at school, so they assumed she must be the same way at home. "She's mean to *me,* but as soon as she meets the other Lakeview kids, she's all smiles. So she's Dr. Jekyll with them, but with me, she's Mr. Hyde."

Sue shrugged and turned back to her meal. Andy didn't know whether she was annoyed at him or what. He decided to drop it.

Soon it was time for the afternoon rehearsal. After the break, the first piece they rehearsed was the Bach double violin concerto.

Andy and the concertmaster walked up to the front of the stage. He hoped he didn't look as scared as his fellow soloist. "Pray a lot," whispered the other boy.

As the orchestra launched into the introduction of the concerto, Andy found that his right hand was aching from clutching his bow so hard. He needed serenity. The thought of serenity suddenly brought a vision of the garden at the Zen Buddhist temple they had visited in Kamakura. The crisp, sharp notes of the music reminded Andy of the sharp rocks in the garden. He found that he was finally able to relax the deathlike grip on his bow. The first solo passage, played by the concertmaster, echoed the orchestral part. Then it was time for Andy's entrance as the second soloist; from his instrument came the same jagged notes, but played in a lower register.

The second movement was the real test for Andy. It opened with his solo, a slow, almost agonizingly beautiful line. Andy thought of the liquid notes of the nightingale at Kencho-ji Temple. Then he remembered the half-closed eyes of the Great Buddha at Kamakura, and he half closed his own eyes. The total calmness in the face of the statue brought him the needed focus. The swirls in his melodic line were like the swirls in the robe of the statue. When he finished his passage, he opened his eyes and glanced up at the conductor. Mr. Baxter was smiling at him.

The concerto was the turning point for the orchestra. The last piece they rehearsed was actually their opening piece for the concert, Schubert's Rosamunde Overture. It was a lively, cheerful piece and a crowd pleaser. True, they played a few wrong notes here and there, but Andy knew the Lakeview orchestra was going to make it.

As the players began to put their instruments away at the end of the rehearsal, the Kasei conductor came up to congratulate the two soloists of the Bach concerto. "Suzuki?" he said, looking at Andy. "You're Japanese, aren't you?"

"No, he's American," Mr. Baxter said firmly.

When Andy met Sue in front of the school, he found that he was starved. He grinned at her. "I need one of Hero's supersized sandwiches, and I need it fast!"

Sue grinned back, and Andy suddenly wished that they could be sitting across from each other at Hero's, just the two of them. Things seemed less complicated there.

The Kasei students began to stream out, and Haruko walked up to Mia. "Goodbye, Mia," she said. "It was so much fun for me to get to talk to some American kids."

"What do you mean?" asked Mia, looking puzzled. "Hasn't Andy been staying with you?"

Haruko flicked a glance at Andy and turned back to Mia. "Well, he's not a *real* American."

Mia's mouth dropped open. "Of course Andy's a real American!" she said. "He's as American as I am!"

"But he can't change his looks, no matter how many years he lives in America," said Haruko with a sniff. "He'll never look completely American."

"Look, Haru . . . uh . . ." Mia paused and took a breath. "Americans come in all shapes and colors. We don't all look exactly the same."

Andy thought the orchestra had done pretty well on Friday afternoon, so he was surprised at how picky Mr. Baxter was when they rehearsed on Saturday morning. He made them play some passages four or five times. He even criticized the concertmaster, who normally played faultlessly. Andy couldn't hear anything wrong with the concertmaster's playing, and he dreaded what Mr. Baxter would say when it was his turn.

Sure enough, when Andy started playing his solo in the second movement of the Bach concerto, Mr. Baxter pounced on him. "Smoother, smoother!" he shouted. "This is supposed to be legato, for God's sake!"

Andy half shut his eyes again and tried to picture the calm face of the Great Buddha. Mr. Baxter's voice seemed to come from a distance, and Andy played almost in a daze. He just hoped he could recover his serenity on the day of the concert.

When Mr. Baxter finally called an end to the

rehearsal, the players were close to collapse. Andy saw that Laurie was almost in tears.

Mr. Baxter cleared his throat. "Well, folks, you probably thought I was a bit hard on you."

There were groans from the players. "We weren't all that bad, were we?" asked a trombone player.

"You weren't bad at all," said Mr. Baxter. "In fact, if you play as well as this at the concert, you'll be okay!" When some of the players started to protest, Mr. Baxter raised his voice. "I was hard on you because this is my last opportunity to really pick on you."

"Aren't we going to rehearse this afternoon?" asked one of the players.

"There's school on Saturday morning, but not in the afternoon," explained Mr. Baxter. "So we can do what we want for the rest of the day. My advice to you is to take it easy and get some rest. God knows I can use some myself!"

"What about tomorrow?" asked Mia. "Aren't we going to rehearse?"

Mr. Baxter shook his head. "Tomorrow is Sunday, and the school is closed all day. That's when you get your chance to do some sightseeing in Tokyo. So have a good time, folks, and I'll see you on Monday! We'll have a short and sweet rehearsal in the morning, and then we wow them at our concert in the evening."

Andy wasn't going to argue with Mr. Baxter. After that rough rehearsal, he wanted to spend the rest of the day as a couch potato—a mashed potato. As the kids left the auditorium, he asked Sue what she planned to do on her free afternoon.

"I'm going to take Mr. Baxter's advice," she said, and smothered a yawn. "I'll just stay at the Chongs', write postcards, and catch up on sleep. That's about all I'm good for. What about you?"

"It depends on the Satos, I guess," said Andy. Too bad he couldn't invite Sue over to be his fellow potato. "I'll have to ask Haruko what her plans are this afternoon."

After lunch, Mrs. Sato apologized to Andy. "I'm sorry, Andy-kun, but Haruko won't be able to take you sightseeing this afternoon. She has to go to school."

"I thought there's no school on Saturday afternoons," said Andy.

"It's a special school that will help Haruko with her mathematics and social studies," explained Mrs. Sato.

Andy was surprised. "Isn't Haruko doing well in school? She seems pretty sharp to me."

Mrs. Sato explained. "Haruko will soon be taking her entrance examinations for college. We want her to do really well." She looked curiously at him. "Don't you have examinations for colleges in America?"

"We do," said Andy. "They're called SATs, or Scholastic Aptitude Tests. The test results help colleges decide whether to accept us—that, plus our grades."

Mrs. Sato nodded. "It's the same in Japan. We all want our children to go to the best schools."

Andy knew that in America some colleges had more prestige than others—the Ivy League schools, for instance. But he didn't personally know of anybody going to a special cram school. The competition seemed to be tougher in Japan.

As Andy watched Haruko glumly walking out the front door, he began to feel a little sorry for her—a little, but not much. At least he wouldn't have to look at her scowling face all afternoon.

He took a long, refreshing nap, and when he woke up he called Sue to see how she was doing. Her voice sounded a bit groggy when she answered. "I just woke up from a nap. How about you? Is Haruko going to take you around?"

"Haruko is going to a special cram school this afternoon," Andy told Sue. "It's to help her with the entrance exams for college. There's cutthroat competition to get into the good ones."

They talked a little more, and Andy finally hung up. He stared at the phone and suddenly felt a strong urge to see Sue's face, to see that mischievous little smile . . . *Hey, what if I go out on my own and look for Sue? Maybe I can call her again and ask for directions to the Chongs' house.*

Then he looked at his watch and saw that it was already four o'clock. It might take him hours to find the right subway and buses to take, and even if he found the right street, he wouldn't recognize the house. He sighed. It just wasn't going to happen.

After hanging up, Sue suddenly had a strong desire to see Andy. Mrs. Chong was out giving music lessons, and Mr. Chong was working at his convenience store. *What if I go out on my own and look for him at the Satos'? Maybe I can call him again and ask for the address.*

But she realized that it would take too long to figure out the right trains and buses to take. She sighed. It just wasn't going to happen.

Well, at least she could take a little walk—go down the street, look around the neighborhood, maybe drop in at Mr. Chong's store.

She put on her shoes and stepped outside. She was immediately hit by a blast of heat, and almost changed her mind and went back in. *Better get used to it, I guess. It's not getting any cooler.*

She opened the gate and walked out into the street. Down the block she found Mr. Chong's convenience store. She went inside and was greeted with a big smile by Mr. Chong. "So you found my place! I'm so sorry that my wife and I can't take you around sightseeing."

"That's all right," said Sue. "I think looking around the neighborhood is just as much fun."

"So what do you think of this place?" asked Mr. Chong. "Is it very different from an American convenience store?"

"Well, your store is much bigger," said Sue, looking around. The convenience stores she knew back home were mostly attached to gas stations. What impressed Sue were the big stacks of boxes containing prepared meals. "These packaged meals look a lot fancier than the frozen TV dinners we get in America," Sue told Mr. Chong.

"Some of my customers come here every night," said Mr. Chong. "They pick up their dinner on their way home from work."

"I guess in America, you drop into a supermarket on your way home from work," said Sue.

"That's because most Americans drive," said Mr. Chong. "Very few people drive in Tokyo, so having a convenience store near your house is very helpful."

Mr. Chong was right, thought Sue. It was late afternoon, and the store was full of people buying their evening meals. Mr. Chong chatted and joked with his customers, clearly enjoying himself.

After a few minutes, Sue left the store and walked around, looking at the small shops nearby. It felt very different from visiting the famous sites in Kamakura. She was looking at an ordinary Japanese neighborhood, with normal people going about their business. At first, because of all the Asian faces around her, the neighborhood reminded her of Chinatown in Seattle.

She passed lots of vending machines on the sidewalk. They sold coffee, both hot and iced, as well as all sorts of teas. She saw soft drinks, familiar and unfamiliar. One was called—no kidding—Pocari Sweat! But what really surprised her was a machine selling liquor, hard liquor. A toddler could put some coins in and walk off with a big bottle of whiskey. *I guess underage drinking must not be as big a problem in Japan as it is in the States.*

She looked into a store renting videos, and the pictures of movie stars she recognized from Hollywood made her feel at home. Then she saw that the titles were all in Japanese. At a magazine store, she was glad to see familiar covers such as *Time* and *Newsweek*. But here, too, the writing was all in Japanese. That was when Sue began to feel very much like a foreigner. Did Andy also feel like a foreigner, or did he feel more at home here? It suddenly became important for Sue to know.

Then she had an idea. *Tomorrow is Sunday, and we have the whole day free. Maybe Andy and I can go around Tokyo, just the two of us!*

Returning to the Chong residence, Sue immediately called Andy. "Tomorrow Mr. and Mrs. Chong are both busy again. Mr. Chong runs a convenience store that stays open on Sundays, and Mrs. Chong will still be giving music lessons."

"Must be boring for you," said Andy. "I'm sitting around watching TV. You know what? They don't have English subtitles!"

Sue laughed at the indignation in Andy's voice. "I took a little walk by myself," she told him, "and it was fun. So why don't the two of us go around Tokyo together tomorrow? We don't have to do anything special, just look around, maybe window-shop, whatever . . ."

"Yeah, let's do that!" cried Andy. Sue could tell he was excited. "There's no rule that says we have to go around with our host families!"

"Maybe we can even find a deli like Hero's where we can hang out," said Sue.

"We'll manage!" said Andy. "I can speak a little bit of Japanese, and you can read some of the signs, the ones written in Chinese characters."

"Great!" said Sue. "I'll ask Mrs. Chong to show me how to get to the Satos' tomorrow morning, and we'll go on from there!"

She could hardly wait for tomorrow.

On Sunday morning, Mrs. Chong insisted on bringing Sue to the Satos' house rather than letting her take her chances alone. The two of them had to take both the subway and a bus. When they got off at the bus stop, Sue could tell immediately that the Satos' house was in a much fancier neighborhood than the Chongs'. The houses were much farther apart, and hidden by tall fences. Walking in the street, Sue felt as if she was being shut out of the lives of the inhabitants. *In America, only rich celebrities cut themselves off like this.*

When Mrs. Chong rang the bell at the gate, Sue began to worry, remembering what Mrs. Chong had told her about the treatment of Koreans by native Japanese. She would never forgive herself if Mrs. Chong was treated rudely. But it was too late to do anything. The gate opened, and a petite, pretty, middle-aged Japanese woman greeted them.

From Mrs. Chong's greeting, Sue guessed that this was Mrs. Sato. And as far as she could tell from the polite bows on both sides, their reception was friendly enough. She felt the tension drain from her shoulders. Things were even better when they stepped into the house—removing her shoes had become automatic by now for Sue—and were greeted by Mr. Sato.

To Sue's relief, he addressed them in English. "Ah, Mrs. Chong! So good to see you. I heard your daughter play last year and was very impressed. She has graduated, yes?"

"Yes, and she is now attending the Toho School of Music," Mrs. Chong said.

"You must be very proud!" said Mr. Sato. His voice sounded wistful.

"Haruko is still not interested in playing an instrument?" Mrs. Chong asked.

"I'm afraid not," said Mr. Sato. "Maybe she can marry a musician, and then we can adopt him into the family."

Sue's mouth dropped open, and she had to force herself to politely shut it. *Haruko can marry a musician? Wow, does he have any particular musician in mind?* Sue couldn't tell whether he was serious or not, but it was clear that Mr. Sato had a deep love of music. *He's being really nice to*

Mrs. Chong. That shows that a person's ancestry doesn't make a difference to him when it comes to music.

"Hey, Sue," said Andy's voice. He appeared in the entryway, carrying his backpack and a guidebook. "All set to go see the sights of Tokyo?"

"I sure am. Andy, this is my hostess, Mrs. Chong. Mrs. Chong, this is my boyfriend, Andy." Sue stepped back and smiled as Andy and Mrs. Chong exchanged a handshake and polite greetings. After thanking Mr. and Mrs. Sato for taking care of Sue, Mrs. Chong bowed and left.

"All set?" Sue asked Andy.

"We have to wait for Haruko," said Andy. "She's coming with us."

Sue's heart sank. She had been so looking forward to some time alone with Andy! "But we can manage on our own!" she protested.

"Haruko is hostess," insisted Mrs. Sato. "It is her duty to go with you."

"I'm sure Haruko has more important things to do," said Sue politely, still not giving up.

"There is nothing more important than showing her guest famous Tokyo sights," said Mrs. Sato.

"Haruko can't be happy about this," Sue whispered to Andy. "If she's already rude to you, imagine what she'll be like when she learns she has to entertain you and your dorky girlfriend. She's going to throw a fit when she sees me."

Andy bent his head to inspect his digital camera. "It's no use. I already tried talking to them."

Fortunately, Haruko didn't keep them waiting too

long. Just a couple of minutes later, she shuffled over to the entryway, munching on a piece of toast. Her expression when she saw Sue was pleasant enough. "Good morning. So you're coming with us?"

Sue blinked. "Uh, yeah. I hope you don't mind having me along, too."

"No, of course not," said Haruko. She didn't look at all angry. "Ready to go?"

By the time they hit the streets, it was already hot. Seeing Haruko put on a small canvas hat, Sue decided that one of the first things she wanted to do was buy a hat for herself. "Can we go to a department store?" she asked.

Haruko's face brightened. "Of course! I take you to my favorite store!"

Sue glanced at Andy and saw that he didn't exactly look psyched about going to a department store. "Isn't it nice that Haruko's in a good mood, at least?" she whispered to him. He just grunted.

The bus they had to take was crowded, even though it was Sunday. "That's when stores are busiest," Haruko told Sue. "Schools, banks, and government offices are all closed, so everybody's shopping."

After the bus, they got on a train, which was less crowded. As the train started, Sue looked around at the other passengers. When she had come into Tokyo from the airport with the Chongs, she had been too tired to notice much.

Many of the seated passengers were typing into their cell phones. "Why do they do that?" Sue asked Haruko.

"In trains we have to use our cell phones silently,"

explained Haruko. "It's called the manner mode, because it's rude to talk into your cell phone in a crowded train."

"Wow," Sue muttered to Andy. "Wish we had rules like that back home." She felt a touch on her arm.

"We get off at the next stop," said Haruko.

It was a good thing Haruko gave them plenty of warning, because it took an effort to push their way to the door through the crowd.

They followed Haruko up some stairs. Sue saw lines on the ground with bumps on them. "What are those for?" she asked Haruko.

"They're for blind people to feel their way," said Haruko. "So they know where they're going."

Outside the train station they were hit by a blast of hot air, but by then Sue was getting used to the weather. They went down a crowded sidewalk, and Sue would have liked to take some time to window-shop. But Haruko kept them marching on.

On the sidewalk, Sue again saw yellow strips with bumps on them to guide the blind. At a busy intersection, she heard music. When the light changed, she heard a different tune. She looked at Andy and saw that he had noticed it, too.

"I've been to cities where you only get a beep when the light changes to guide the blind," said Andy. "Light signals with songs are better!"

"Here!" cried Haruko. "In here!"

Sue and Andy followed her through revolving doors and found themselves in blessed air-conditioning. To

Sue, the interior didn't look all that different from that of an American department store. The lighting, the counters, and even the merchandise looked similar. One difference was a young woman in uniform standing at the foot of the escalator, bowing and greeting all the customers.

"Hats on third floor," Haruko said.

They took the escalator to the third floor, where hats, gloves, scarves, and other accessories were. Sue looked at some of the prices and shuddered. There was no way she could afford this stuff. Did Haruko think all Americans were rich?

The hat department had a huge selection, but after looking at the prices, Sue settled on the simplest one she could find, a khaki canvas hat with a narrow brim.

"Why don't we go to the top of the store and then work our way down, one floor at a time," suggested Haruko.

Sue glanced at Andy. She knew he wasn't exactly a shopaholic, so this wasn't much fun for him.

"A quick pass through," Andy agreed. "Sure. But let's not spend all day here. We can shop in Seattle."

"Can we at least look at traditional Japanese clothes, like kimonos and stuff?" Sue asked. "That's something we won't see in Seattle."

"All right, if you really want to," said Haruko. She sounded less than enthusiastic.

They traveled to a floor with kimonos and all their accessories. These included special underwear, and narrow sashes that were invisible from the outside but were needed to hold things in place. Just the footwear that went with the kimono needed a whole department to itself.

Sue looked at the prices. She converted to dollars and nearly choked when she discovered that a whole outfit would cost many thousands of dollars. "Do you wear a kimono often?" she asked Haruko.

"Only once or twice a year," said Haruko. "On New Year's Day, I wear a kimono and go with my parents to a shrine. But it's such a pain! It takes hours to get dressed in a kimono!"

Sue looked at all the shiny silk. Some kimonos had gold or silver threads woven into them. "They're gorgeous," she murmured. For a moment, she felt envious.

"Don't you wear Chinese clothes?" asked Haruko. "Some of them are beautiful! I've seen cheongsams with gorgeous embroidery."

Sue glanced at Haruko. When the Japanese girl didn't have her usual sullen expression, she wasn't bad-looking at all. She had neat, dark brows above eyes that were now bright and interested. Sue realized that Haruko didn't seem to feel the prejudice against the Chinese that Mrs. Chong had talked about. In fact, Haruko was a lot more friendly to *her* than to Andy.

"No, I don't get to wear a cheongsam," Sue told Haruko. "My grandmother gave me one, but I outgrew it a long time ago. The cheongsam is a tight fit, not like a kimono."

Andy was fidgeting and shuffling his feet. "Come on, let's keep going. I've had enough of kimonos."

Sue grinned at him. "I thought you'd be interested in

your roots. Don't you want to see how your grand-mother dressed?"

"Both my grandmothers are Japanese Americans," said Andy, "and I don't remember ever seeing them wear kimonos."

They went down one floor and found themselves in the gift department. "In August and at New Year, you always buy a gift for your boss," Haruko explained. "So you come here, tell them how much you want to spend, and they send the gift for you. Do you have something like that in America?"

Sue thought about gifts. "Well, when somebody you know is getting married, you go to a store and ask whether your friend has registered, and if they have, you get a whole list of things they've said they want so you'll know exactly what to give them."

"What a weird system!" cried Haruko.

Sue remembered something Mrs. Chong had mentioned. "Is it true that Japanese parents sometimes hire detectives to investigate their children's friends, to see if they're fit for their son or daughter to marry?"

Haruko hesitated. She flicked a glance at Andy before replying. "Well, some old-fashioned parents like to look over their children's future husband or wife." What Haruko did not say was whether her own parents were old-fashioned.

Sue saw that Andy was drifting away again, so they hurried through the next few floors. At last they arrived at the lowest floor, the basement food department, and Andy brightened up. A bunch of counters had free samples, so they helped themselves to bite-sized pieces of pastry, pickled eggplant, smoked fish . . . plus things Sue had never seen before. Some of the samples were delicious, and Sue sneaked back to take another piece. Some were very strange.

"Okay, we've seen every single floor," said Andy, after they had made the rounds. "Let's go somewhere interesting. What do kids do for fun?"

Haruko thought a bit. "How about going to an arcade?"

"Okay, video games, then," said Andy. "Let's go!"

Haruko took them to an arcade, and Sue saw that many of the games didn't look that different from the ones back home. Andy walked over to one and immediately started shooting down enemy aliens.

Sue found the game boring and glanced at Haruko. She was staring straight at Andy. Suddenly Sue wondered whether Andy was trying to impress Haruko. She remembered what Andy had written on the wooden plaque at the shrine in Kamakura.

Is Andy trying to impress Haruko because she's cold to him? Maybe he likes the challenge?

Sue knew she was being unreasonable—Haruko lived thousands of miles away from Andy, and she knew Andy didn't like her much as a person. Still, something rankled about the way Andy tried so hard to gain Haruko's respect. Sue turned away.

Soon Andy was done and he looked at other games. There was one that Sue had seen in America where the player had to dance according to the rhythm and choreography dictated by the machine. If he got out of step, a loud beep sounded.

"This looks like fun," said Andy.

The music started. Watching Andy keeping up with the flashing video game, Sue suddenly realized that they had never danced together. He was good! His shoulders moved in the sexy way she'd first noticed during her audition at the Lakeview auditorium. Sue wished desperately that the two of them could go someplace where they could really dance, *without* Haruko.

There was a loud beep. Andy laughed and stopped dancing. "Good thing Mr. Baxter doesn't make that noise when I play the wrong note."

Andy turned to another game, but it had a line of customers waiting. In fact, there were people waiting to play at most of the machines.

Sue had had enough of the game arcade. "We might as well be doing this back home."

When they emerged blinking from the dark arcade into the too-bright street, they found that it was past noon. Having eaten all those samples in the department store, Sue didn't feel very hungry. "I could head over to some coffee shop and have a drink," she said. "How about you guys?"

Andy, who had helped himself to the most samples, agreed. He suddenly pointed. "Hey, there's a Starbucks over there!"

Sue felt a sudden stab of nostalgia but fought it down. They had not come to Tokyo to have coffee at Starbucks. "Aren't there Japanese coffee shops, too?" she asked Haruko.

"Of course there are!" snapped Haruko. "We had coffee shops long before you had Starbucks."

They followed Haruko to the next block, where they found a café with dishes of food displayed in the window: spaghetti, hamburgers with French fries, a plate of yellow rice with little bits of stuff embedded, and tiny sandwiches with the crusts cut off. Haruko told them the display was made of plastic, but the food looked very realistic.

They sat down at a corner table and ordered some drinks. Andy ordered a cup of coffee, while Sue ordered one of the bubble teas, a tall, milky drink containing little balls of tapioca. She looked around at the walls, which had posters of comic book characters. "I recognize some of these manga characters."

"Do you have manga in America?" asked Haruko.

"Of course we do!" said Sue. "Comics started in America."

"Actually, comics started in Japan," said Andy. "According to my dad, a Japanese artist painted a series of comic episodes, which he titled 'Animal Frolics.' The artist was a twelfth-century monk living in Kyoto."

Sue's astonishment was nothing compared to Haruko's. The Japanese girl's jaw dropped, and she stared at Andy as if seeing him for the first time. "Your father knows Japanese paintings?" she asked Andy.

"Sure!" said Andy. "He likes black-and-white ink paintings the best." He smiled at Sue as he added, "Like your mother's paintings."

As Haruko thoughtfully sipped her drink, Sue studied the menu posted above the counter. She suddenly realized something. "Hey! Most of the items are in English!"

Before coming to Japan, Andy had taught Sue to read katakana. It was one of the two Japanese phonetic writing systems, the one used to write all foreign expressions. The katakana system has only forty-six symbols to learn. Sue was able to learn them and sound out words after only a couple of days.

Now, looking at the menu, Sue began to pronounce the words. *"Aisu kurimu,"* she read. "It means ice cream!" she cried triumphantly.

Andy studied the menu. "You're right! *Kohi* must be coffee, so *kohi miruku* must be coffee milk, or latte!"

It was fun. Sue immediately got *hamu sandoichi,* ham sandwich, but she had trouble with *omuraisu.* Andy laughed and pointed to the next table, where a woman was eating some rice covered with egg. "It's omelet rice," he said.

But *kare raisu* baffled even Andy, until Haruko explained that it meant curry rice. Sue realized that it must have been that plate of yellow rice she had seen in the window.

Sue and Andy had great fun translating the rest of the menu, but Haruko was not amused. "You make fun of Japanese because we use foreign words. But you do, too. Isn't latte Italian?"

Andy raised his hands in surrender. "Okay, okay. We're all guilty." He looked around the coffee shop. "You know, I'm getting a little tired of modern Tokyo. I don't really feel that this"—he pointed at the espresso machine, the ham sandwiches, the plates of spaghetti, the Anglicized menu—"is where my people originally came from. Where's the *real* Japan?"

"What do you mean by the *real* Japan?" demanded Haruko. "You mean you want to see scenes from a samurai movie? If that's what you want, we'd better go to the Toho movie studio. They have tours, you know."

"I just want to see what's typically Japanese," muttered Andy.

"Then tell me what's typically American," said Haruko. "Cowboys and Indians?"

Somewhat to her surprise, Sue found herself siding with Haruko. "Some tourists going to China think that old women with bound feet sitting around playing mahjongg is typical."

"Maybe what I really want is to see the things my father likes to talk about," said Andy.

"All right," said Haruko, sounding a little calmer. "What sort of Japanese things does your father talk about?"

Andy was silent as he thought. He added more sugar to his coffee and stirred. "The more traditional things, I guess."

Sue suddenly remembered a picture she had seen in a travel magazine. She turned to Haruko. "There's this Buddhist temple with a huge paper lantern. I thought it looked amazing. Do you know the one I mean?"

"I think you mean Asakusa Temple," said Haruko. "But it's in an old-fashioned part of town."

"An old-fashioned part of town is exactly what I want to see," Andy said quickly.

"Oh, all right," sighed Haruko. She didn't seem at all enthusiastic. "We'll have to take the subway. Let's go."

12

andy found the Tokyo subway system really easy to use. There were diagrams at all the stations, with the name of each stop as well as the names of the previous stop and the next stop. Haruko nudged them to get out at the Asakusa station.

The minute they hit the street, Andy felt a different vibe. Here, the streets were narrower and more crooked, and were lined with smaller shops. Instead of big, modern multistory buildings with huge glass windows, the buildings here were mostly one or two stories. It was as crowded as the modern area, but here the crowd seemed to move more slowly. Another difference was that most of the people were either old or very young.

"I guess teenagers don't hang out here much?" asked Andy.

Haruko sniffed. "Too many country people here."

Andy frowned. *I guess a sophisticated city girl like you wouldn't want to be caught dead in a neighborhood full of country people.*

Haruko led them to a long pedestrian walk lined with stalls on either side. "This is Nakamise," she said. "It leads to Asakusa Temple."

The stalls were selling a multitude of objects, some familiar, some unfamiliar. There were paper fans, spinning tops, pencil cases, wooden swords . . .

Andy grinned when he saw a stall selling goldfish from a tank, and a little kid trying to catch one with a scoop made of paper. "Hey, I remember my dad telling me about this!"

"How can that kid possibly catch a goldfish that way?" asked Sue. "The paper will break up in the water."

Andy watched the unsuccessful efforts of the little kid. "You have to be really good to catch the fish before the paper breaks."

He decided to try for a goldfish. It was harder than he thought, but on his third try, he did it! The man at the stall handed him his goldfish in a little plastic bag full of water.

"How are you going to get that fish past security at the airport?" asked Sue. "They'll think it's some sort of new weapon."

Andy laughed. He presented his prize to the little boy who hadn't been able to catch a fish. He could have spent all day browsing along the Nakamise. It was a lot more fun than looking at dresses in a department store.

He heard a gasp from Sue. "Look at that gate!"

In front of them was the main gate of the Asakusa Temple. They stared, stunned by the sheer size of the gate and the paper lantern. Andy, who was taller than average in Japan, now felt like a midget.

Sue broke the silence. "It's way more impressive in real life."

Andy took his camera out of his backpack. "Can you stand over there, under the lantern?" he said to Sue and Haruko.

He snapped several pictures of the two girls by the gate, then took several of them in front of the main hall of the temple, and a few more next to the pagoda. Haruko began to object. "I didn't know you even had a camera. Why didn't you take pictures earlier?"

"I didn't need pictures of stores and arcades and coffee shops," said Andy, who thought the answer was obvious. "I want to bring home pictures of . . . of . . ."

"Pictures of the *real* Japan," said Haruko, sneering. "Pictures of what you heard your father talk about. Just like tourists in America want pictures of cowboys and Indians."

Here we go again. But Andy was too interested in the neighborhood to waste time fighting with Haruko. "Come on, let's explore."

As they wandered through the narrow streets, Andy saw an old woman wearing a plain blue and white cotton kimono. The kimono was nothing like the brightly colored silk ones they had seen in the department store.

The old woman wore white cotton socks, and her feet were thrust into *zori*, thong sandals. She walked in small steps, with her feet pointing slightly inward. Andy couldn't resist taking a picture of someone who looked like, well, his great-grandmother—or what he imagined his great-grandmother to be.

A teenage boy hurried up to the old woman and handed her a small wrapped package. "Here you are, Grandma," he said. At least that was what Andy thought it sounded like. Then the boy opened up a parasol and held it over his grandmother's head as they walked.

"Did you see that?" Andy whispered to Sue, pointing at the two figures. He couldn't picture himself going out on a Sunday afternoon with his grandmother. But he could picture Sue walking with her grandmother, holding a parasol over her head. *I've got to figure out a way to deal with Sue's grandma.*

"Soup!" Sue suddenly yelled.

Andy turned and saw that she was pointing at two wooden doors with big Chinese characters painted on them.

"Why are there separate doors for men and women, if they're going in there to have soup?" asked Sue.

Haruko broke into giggles. Andy peered at the characters and tried to remember the lessons he had taken years earlier. Suddenly he understood, and started laughing, too. "This is *yu*, the character for hot water, not soup," he told Sue. "So we're looking at a public bathhouse, not a soup kitchen."

"Oh," said Sue in a small voice. "Well, this is the character I learned in my Chinese class for 'soup.' I guess the characters changed meaning when they were exported to Japan."

"Or they could have changed meaning in China, and stayed the same in Japan," said Andy. "Hey, want to try this public bath?"

Sue grinned. "But there are separate baths for men and women. That's no fun!"

Haruko spoke up. "These public baths are used by mostly *neighborhood* people, and not by many strangers."

The way Haruko emphasized the word "neighborhood" reminded Andy of something his mother had told him: in feudal days, Tokyo was divided into two parts. The Upper Town was occupied by the shogun, lords, and samurai. The Lower Town was occupied by shopkeepers and workers. Since the Satos were descended from a samurai family, Andy suspected that Haruko was reluctant to visit this neighborhood not only because it was old-fashioned, but also because it was in the Lower Town. As they turned a corner, Andy smelled something like burnt sugar. It came from a little cart pushed by a skinny old man. Andy suddenly realized that he was hungry. It had been a long time since they had eaten the samples in the department store. "What is he selling?" he asked, pointing to the cart.

"Roasted yams," said Haruko, wrinkling her nose. "I haven't had them for years."

Andy associated roasted yams with Thanksgiving dinners. Although the smell was tantalizing, he was too hungry for yams. "Let's look for someplace to have lunch."

A couple of blocks down, they came to a street lined

with cafés, mostly tiny places serving a dozen people, tops. There were plastic displays in the windows, but Andy could see that the dishes were different from the ones in the trendy Shibuya café. Instead of dainty sandwiches, spaghetti, and hamburgers and French fries, the displays here were mostly noodle soup, fried noodles, or rice dishes.

In one of the eateries, Andy saw the yellow *kare raisu*, curry rice. He wanted to give it a try. "Let's go in here," he said to Sue.

Haruko made a face but followed them in. It was a tiny place, with barely enough room to maneuver in. They inserted themselves into some seats and gave their orders.

The two girls ordered soup noodles. "I want to try some ramen that isn't instant," said Sue.

Sue's bowl of noodles turned out to look so good that Andy was sorry he had ordered the curry rice, especially when he discovered that the little brown chunks in his rice turned out not to be meat but something rubbery. Sue and Haruko busily slurped their noodles. Andy knew that if Sue had been eating spaghetti in Hero's, she wouldn't be slurping. But here in Tokyo, it felt right—especially when a really loud slurp reached his ears from the table behind him.

"Do the Chinese slurp when they eat noodles?" he asked Sue, before he could stop himself.

Sue looked up from her bowl and grinned at him. "Of course! We *invented* the slurp."

"Sure, sure," said Andy, "just like you invented everything else."

"Paper, printing, gunpowder . . . you name it," said Sue. From her bowl she picked up a small slice of something striped in pink and white. "What's this? Whatever it is, it tastes good."

"It's made of fish paste," said Haruko, whose soup noodles contained slices of barbecued pork. "I don't like it very much."

"Because it's traditional, right?" said Andy. It bugged him how Haruko automatically put down anything traditionally Japanese.

Haruko threw down her chopsticks with a clatter. "Look, I know you were hoping to see the Japan your father described. But we can't stay the same forever, you know. America has changed, so why can't Japan change, too?"

Andy poked at his plate of curry rice. He struggled to put his thoughts into words. "Look, I'm not saying that I expect Japan to be like a museum," he said finally. "You have new things, cell phones, video game arcades, shopping malls, and stuff. I'm okay with that. But what I don't like is the way you want to throw *away* all the old stuff. Don't you care about your cultural heritage at all?"

The minute he used the phrase "cultural heritage," Andy realized that he sounded like his social studies teacher. From the smile on Sue's face, he saw that she realized it, too.

Haruko picked up her chopsticks again and fished around in her bowl for stray bits of pork. After a moment she looked up at Andy. She seemed genuinely puzzled. "You mean you *want* to think about your Japanese heritage, even when you're living in America?" she asked.

"Yes, I do," said Andy. When he returned home, he wanted to bring with him memories of the Satos' Japanese-style garden, the calm face of the Buddha at Kamakura, and the huge lantern at the Asakusa Temple.

"I think about my Chinese heritage a lot," said Sue. "We eat Chinese food at home, mostly. My mother insists that I learn some Chinese writing, too. In fact, knowing Chinese characters has been pretty useful here in Japan."

"Except when you're wondering why there are separate soups for men and women," said Andy. He and Sue grinned at each other.

Haruko suddenly broke in. "I think the reason we don't talk about our cultural heritage is because we're surrounded by it! But you keep thinking about your Asian cultural heritage because you're a Japanese American, surrounded by real Americans."

Andy had to bite his lip to keep from saying something nasty. *Real Americans? How many more times am I going to have to hear that?* Haruko had obviously been hoping to get a white kid from Lakeview, instead of a Japanese American like himself. To her, he was only a second-rate American, and she felt cheated. "Haruko, Americans—*real* Americans—come in all sizes and colors!" he snapped.

Haruko just looked at him blankly over her soup. Andy could see that he hadn't convinced her. To her, he wasn't a real American, and he wasn't a satisfactory Japanese, either. He wore his toilet slippers into the rest of the house and put the wrong side of his kimono on top. He was a complete loser, as far as she was concerned.

They ate in silence for a few minutes. Sue turned to look at a table next to theirs, occupied by four teenagers. They were all frantically typing into their cell phones with their thumbs, instead of talking to one another. "Do you send messages to your friends, too?" she asked Haruko.

"Of course! Don't you?" said Haruko.

"Well, I talk to them on my cell phone sometimes," replied Sue, "but typing messages is too much work."

"That's because you have old-fashioned machine. My cell phone is much better," said Haruko triumphantly. She pulled her machine out and showed it to Sue and Andy. He noticed that it had a full keyboard, instead of a number pad that you had to punch several times to get the right letter.

"In some areas we're ahead of you," said Haruko. "See, we don't always copy other countries!"

"Well, I still don't see what's so great about typing messages to my friends when I can just talk to them on the phone," said Sue. "Don't you *talk* to your friends?"

"Sure, at school. But all my friends type messages," said Haruko.

"What happens when someone wants to be different?" asked Andy.

Haruko frowned. "There is old saying in Japan: the nail that sticks up is the one that gets pounded down," she said.

"Well, in America, I guess it's okay to be different, to

stick out," said Andy. "In Japan, you're all descended from the same ancestors, so everyone looks the same. But in America, we're all immigrants."

Haruko shook her head. "*You* are an immigrant, of course, but the white people, the real Americans, are not immigrants!"

Andy felt his face burn with anger. "For your information, Haruko, *everybody* in America is an immigrant, except for the Native Americans. Even *they* came from Asia across the Bering Strait, according to my mother."

His lecture made no impression on Haruko, who continued to look scornful. Andy jerked his thumb at the next table, where three of the four kids had dyed hair. "Why do so many of you dye your hair red, blond, or brown? Is it because you want to look Caucasian? I think it's pathetic!"

Haruko bristled, and even Sue looked embarrassed. "Dyeing our hair is just a fashion," snapped Haruko. "Fashions come and go. Don't you have fads in America, too? I hear that some American kids even have tattoos!"

"You know, I haven't seen any kids with tattoos here," said Sue. "Don't you have them?"

"The *yakuza* have tattoos," said Haruko. "That's why not many kids have them."

"The yakuza are Japanese gangsters," Andy explained to Sue. "They're like the Mafia."

"So you can't even have a tiny little flower tattooed on your ankle?" Sue asked Haruko. "Not even your boyfriend's name, or just 'Mom'?"

"Tattoos are mostly for yakuza," repeated Haruko.

"And Americans have other fads, too, like piercing. They have rings in their ears, nose, lips, or eyebrows."

"Or other places I won't mention," muttered Andy.

"Don't Japanese kids do any piercing?" asked Sue.

"Some do, but my parents wouldn't let me," Haruko said primly. "Besides, our school has a rule against piercing. So if someone has a ring in his nose, he has to take it out for school."

"Things are more uniform here, that's for sure," said Sue. "Maybe that's why there's so much discrimination against immigrants, who are different. My host family, the Chongs, are Korean. They have a hard time living in Japan."

"Why don't they go back to Korea, then?" grumbled Haruko.

Sue shook her head. "Koreans were brought to Japan as forced labor, Mrs. Chong said. They're like the freed African slaves in America, who found that they had no home to return to in Africa."

"Okay, you mention African slaves," crowed Haruko. "So you Americans can't criticize other people for discrimination, when black people have such a bad time in America."

Andy jumped in. "You just called us 'you Americans.' Does that mean you admit that Sue and I are *real* Americans, after all?"

For a few seconds, the three of them just stared at one another, breathing hard. Then Andy and Haruko spoke at the same time. "Peace!" said Haruko, while Andy said, "Truce!"

They all burst out laughing. Finally Andy said, "Come on, let's go and look around some more." He turned to Sue. "You put up with me while I searched for my roots. Now it's *your* turn. What do you want to see?"

Sue gave a grin that was both shy and mischievous, the one that Andy liked so much. "How about searching for *my* roots in that store over there?" She pointed at a big sign over a store across the street. "I recognize those characters. They say 'Chinese Store.' "

The store was huge, and it contained heaps of miscellaneous objects, many of them familiar to Andy from Chinatown back home. It felt strange to be browsing through a Chinese store in Tokyo. He was struck by a sudden idea. While the two girls were busy looking at some brocade jackets, Andy hurried to the toy department.

He had just finished paying for his purchase and having it wrapped when Sue and Haruko came up. "What did you get?" asked Sue.

"It's a surprise," Andy said. To change the subject, he asked quickly, "Can't find anything you like?"

"No point in buying stuff that I can get back home," said Sue.

"Things here are cheap," said Haruko. "They come directly from China."

Sue made a face. "I guess most Chinese things must look cheap to you."

To Andy's surprise, Haruko shook her head. "My father comes here to buy ink stick. He said the best ink stick he ever found was from this store."

In addition to the Chinese store, the street had a number of small shops selling a variety of hardware.

They walked past an area Haruko called Kimchee Alley, kimchee being Korean pickled cabbage. Andy could detect a strong smell of garlic in the air. *I guess this neighborhood must still be the Lower Town for the underprivileged, since it contains second-class citizens like the Chinese, the Koreans, and old women who look like my great-grandmother.*

Farther down the block, Andy heard clicking and saw a place filled with vertical pinball machines. He remembered his father's description. *"Pachinko!"* he cried.

"What's pachinko?" asked Sue.

"'Pachinko' means pinball machine," explained Andy. "Only the panels are vertical, instead of horizontal. My dad says it's hugely popular in Japan. If you win, you can get all sorts of prizes, like cigarettes, candy, liquor, and stuff."

He turned to Sue. "Let's go in and try our luck."

Haruko hung back. "I don't think it's a good idea. Kids aren't allowed, anyway."

Andy was confident that he was tall enough to pass for an adult. "Okay, if you don't want to go in," he said to Haruko, "then Sue and I are going in and you can wait outside. We'll just be a minute."

Andy went to the cashier, who didn't seem to care about his age, and paid for a container of little steel balls. Then he seated himself at a vacant machine and began to feed the balls in and pull the lever. He sent the little balls whizzing through their paths. They all disappeared.

Sue, who was watching a man playing at another machine, said to Andy, "I think you need skill, not luck." A whirring noise sounded, and a cascade of little balls fell into the man's dish. With hardly a pause, he began to feed some of the balls back into the machine. Soon, another cascade of balls fell into his dish.

Andy was beginning to think Sue was right. He went back to the cashier and paid for some more balls. But he had no better luck on his next try. He used up his batch of balls without getting any back. "I've had better luck at slot machines," he said with a sigh.

Haruko had been fidgeting at the entrance. She stepped forward and whispered nervously, "Come on, let's go!" Without waiting for his reply, she turned abruptly and bumped into a man carrying a container of balls. Some of the balls fell on the ground and scattered.

The man grabbed Haruko by the arm and began to snarl curses. At least, they sounded like curses. Andy didn't know any of the words.

Haruko tried to pull away, but the man's grip only tightened. As he extended his arm, his tattoos became visible. Andy felt a chill down his spine. *The yakuza!* Without giving himself time to think, he got up and ran over to the man. "Let her go," he said in Japanese, narrowing his eyes and making his voice as menacing as possible.

"I'm all right, Andy," gasped Haruko. But she looked scared to death.

"For the last time," Andy said between his teeth, "let her go!"

"What's going on?" said Sue, rushing over. She spoke in English.

Startled, the tattooed man turned to Sue. "American?" he asked.

In his surprise, the man's grip loosened, and Haruko wrenched her arm free. She poured a torrent of words at the man, of which Andy understood only a few, "guests," and "visitors from America."

The man grunted something, turned his back on them, and began to pick up his scattered balls.

"Let's go," hissed Haruko. Andy and Sue didn't need any urging. They quickly followed Haruko out into the street.

They hurried down the block, and slowed only when they could no longer see the sign of the pachinko parlor. Andy wiped the sweat from his eyes. "Yakuza?" he asked.

"Yes," said Haruko in a low voice. "Many pachinko parlors controlled by the yakuza. That's another reason I didn't want to go there."

Andy shook his head. "That's something my dad didn't tell me." After a moment, he added, "You know, I think I've seen enough of the Lower Town."

Sue looked at her watch. "It's getting late, anyway. We'd better head back. I don't want to keep Mrs. Chong waiting."

As they made their way to the train station, Haruko turned to Andy. "Thank you for helping me, Andy. That was very brave."

"Not brave," muttered Andy, shuddering as he thought of what the yakuza member might have done to him. "Just plain stupid."

He sighed. He had finally gained Haruko's respect— but not quite the way he had planned.

13

When the Lakeview players met at the school on Monday, they had so much to say to each other about their day off that Mr. Baxter gave up trying to get the rehearsal started. He realized that he had to let them talk themselves out first.

Nathan was showing off a handheld game he had bought in Akihabara, a neighborhood with lots of electronics stores. Laurie told Andy her host family had taken her to Yokohama. "We rode the Bullet Train," she said. "The whole trip lasted about fifteen minutes, and we arrived before I knew we had even left Tokyo!"

Andy was envious. "One of the things I wanted to do

in Japan was take the Bullet Train. My dad told me so much about it."

"The train we took, the Kodama, wasn't even the fastest train," said Laurie. "The Hikari is faster, and the Nozomi is the fastest of all. But they go on different lines."

"What did you do in Yokohama?" asked Sue, coming over. "It's the port city for Tokyo, isn't it?"

"Yeah, it's where all the big ocean liners come in," said Laurie. "But guess what? We ate lunch in Chinatown! Yokohama has the biggest Chinatown in Japan."

There were squeals from some of the girls. Ginny was waving a silk scarf she had bought at a store in Ginza. "Ginza is like Fifth Avenue, Rodeo Drive, and Bond Street all rolled into one!" she was saying breathlessly.

Andy caught Sue's eye. "I've heard of Fifth Avenue and Rodeo Drive, but what's Bond Street?" he asked.

Sue laughed. "Like I'd know! That scarf cost almost ten thousand yen, which is way out of my budget."

"Mine, too," said Andy. He looked curiously at Sue. "Are you sorry we didn't go to Ginza?"

Sue laughed again. "What's the point? There's no fun just salivating."

"So what did you do in Tokyo, Sue?" Ginny asked, coming over. "It must have been a little like coming home for you, right?"

Andy could see the annoyance in Sue's eyes, but she answered in a level voice. "No, Ginny, Tokyo was not like home. I'm *Chinese* American, remember?"

"Oops, sorry!" said Ginny. "But you know what I mean. You don't look any different from the Japanese. Doesn't it make you feel more at home when you look the same as the people around you?"

Sue sighed loudly. "You mean I don't look like a freak here, the way I do in America? Then you'd feel right at home in Moscow, since lots of Russians have blond hair like yours, right?"

"Hair color isn't everything, Ginny," said Mia. "That Japanese girl . . . what's her name . . . Harko . . . *she's* got blond hair, the same color as yours!"

Sue and Mia started to giggle. "Okay, okay," said Ginny. She turned to Andy. "But at least it's like homecoming for *you*, isn't it?"

"No, it isn't," said Andy. "Not really. I feel like a stranger here, too. I made a fool of myself when I almost wore the toilet slippers into the living room."

"What did you do on Sunday, Mia?" asked Sue.

"My host family took me to historical places, like the Meiji Shrine and the Imperial Palace," said Mia. "They thought I'd want to see the most important sites in Tokyo."

"What was the palace like?" asked Nathan. "Was it full of samurai swords and armor? I went to the Tower of London once, and there were these suits of armor all over the place."

"I didn't see any armor," said Mia. "In fact, most of the place was closed to the public. But the gardens were pretty nice."

Listening to all the kids talking about what they had

done, Andy was struck by how completely different their experiences had been. They might have gone to different cities in different countries. Could any of them say that what they had seen was typically Japanese?

He had asked Haruko to take him to the Lower Town so he could see things he thought were part of the *real* Japan. But now he had to admit that Haruko had a point. What the other kids had seen—Ginza, the electronics center, the Imperial Palace, the Bullet Train—they were part of the *real* Japan, too.

Had he found his roots during the trip? No, he had found instead that he was more American than he had realized. He was no more part of this Japan than Sue was part of that Chinese store they had browsed in.

Mr. Baxter finally called his players together, and they filed into the auditorium. The rehearsal was short, because the conductor didn't want to tire them out before the concert that evening. At the end, Mr. Baxter smiled at the orchestra. "Okay, people, just remember to play the same notes again this evening."

"Scared?" Sue asked Andy as they stood in front of the school, waiting to be picked up by their host families.

"Not nearly as scared as I was in that pachinko parlor," said Andy. His heart still skipped a beat every time he thought about the tattooed yakuza.

"All I noticed about the man was that he was missing his little finger on one hand," said Sue, with a shudder. "Haruko told me afterwards that many yakuza cut off their little finger as an apology for doing something wrong."

Andy winced. He was glad he hadn't known about this gruesome custom before. "Can we talk about something else? I need all my fingers to play the violin!"

But he wasn't allowed to forget about the episode in the pachinko parlor. That night, he had dinner one last time with his host family. Instead of sitting on chairs around the dining table, they ate in the Japanese-style room, sitting on the floor around a low table. It was going to be a formal occasion.

When Andy came into the room, Mr. Sato put his hands flat on the floor and bowed to him. Andy was confused. Wasn't *he* supposed to bow to his hosts like that and thank them for their hospitality? He hurriedly got down on the floor and bowed back, as deeply as he could manage. "I thank you for taking me into your home and treating me like a member of the family," he said to the floor, keeping his head an inch above the tatami mat.

"No, it is *I* who must thank *you* for saving our daughter, Haruko, from the yakuza yesterday," said Mr. Sato.

Then, to Andy's intense embarrassment, the elder Mr. Sato and Mrs. Sato bowed to him as well. Haruko sat silent, but she was looking at him with a faint smile. A smile that contained no trace of her former contempt.

Andy cleared his throat. "No, listen. Haruko tried her best to talk me out of going to the pachinko parlor. It was entirely *my* fault that we went there in the first place."

To Andy's relief, all the Satos finally sat up. Mr. Sato smiled. "I'm not talking about why you went to the pachinko parlor. What I'm saying is that you showed real courage in facing the yakuza and telling him to let go of Haruko."

"I didn't know what I was doing," mumbled Andy.

"But you did know that the man was a yakuza, didn't you?" said Haruko.

"Well, to be completely honest, I didn't suspect he was a yakuza until I saw the tattoo," admitted Andy. "By that time, it was too late."

"Even then, you didn't back down," said Haruko. The admiration in her eyes made him blush. He put his finger inside his collar to loosen it. For the concert, he had put on his white shirt and his suit and tie. Even with air-conditioning, he was feeling warm.

Mrs. Sato began to serve dinner. She brought in a separate tray for each person, containing little dishes of various shapes and sizes. Back home, on very special occasions, Andy's parents had taken him to fancy Japanese restaurants where they served food like this. He knew that there would be successive trays coming. There was only a tiny amount of food in each of the dishes, but they were in contrasting shapes and colors. Together, they made a gorgeous arrangement.

Mrs. Sato also brought in a tray with a little white porcelain bottle and tiny stemmed cups. She filled four of the cups and handed them around to her father-in-law, her husband, Haruko, and Andy. He discovered that the liquid served was sake.

"I know that you must not drink too much because of the concert later," said Mr. Sato. "But I should like to give a toast, at least." He raised his cup, and the others followed suit. "To our guest, Andrew Suzuki. Let us hope this first meeting will not be the last."

Andy did his best to think of a graceful reply, but all he could think of was "You have made your house feel like home to me."

At Andy's reply, Haruko broke out into a soft laugh. Both Mr. and Mrs. Sato were beaming. Andy hoped they weren't reading more into his reply than he intended. He felt a strong urge to take off his tie.

They began to eat. Andy tasted some yellowish paste, which Haruko told him was made from sea urchin eggs. It was delicious, and Andy tried not to think about where it came from.

Mr. Sato cleared his throat and looked at Andy. "I confess that I looked over the list of players in the Lakeview orchestra, and when I saw your name, I made inquiries. I was told that you were a most promising player, and that you would be one of the soloists for the Bach concerto."

"So you actually asked to be the host for Andy?" asked Haruko.

"Yes, I asked for Andy specifically," replied Mr. Sato. "And now I see that it was an excellent choice."

Andy knew that many Lakeview orchestra members went to the families they had hosted last year in Seattle, while the rest of the host families had been determined largely by drawing lots. It seemed that someone influential, like Mr. Sato, could choose the player he would host. If Haruko had been given the choice, of course, she would have chosen someone like Mia.

Mr. Sato was studying Andy closely. "The other morning, you said your father tried to teach you to appreciate a Zen garden. It shows taste. And your courage in facing the yakuza, it makes me suspect that your father is descended from a samurai family, perhaps?"

"No, his family were not samurai," Andy said firmly. "They were originally farmers."

"Oh, I see," said Mr. Sato, looking disappointed. He ate some grilled fish and picked at some marinated spinach.

"You can be adopted into a samurai family," said the elder Mr. Sato.

Andy tugged at his collar again. Were the Satos sizing him up as a potential husband for Haruko? He tried to imagine Sue's family grilling him on his background. "Was your grandfather a Mandarin, or did he fail his official examinations?" Sue's mother would ask.

Two more trays followed, each with different kinds of food, and Andy lost count of how many little dishes he ate from. He looked at Mrs. Sato and wondered how she could have prepared this feast and still looked so elegant. "I hope you didn't go to too much trouble," he told her.

Haruko laughed. "Mother ordered the food sent from a local restaurant," she explained.

Andy blushed and went back to eating. He stole a look at Haruko and realized that when she stopped sulking, she could be quite attractive. He couldn't help comparing her to Sue. Both girls were slight in build, and both moved gracefully. The main difference was probably in personality. Haruko was eager to keep up with the latest fashion, but Sue was happy to go her own way. That was one of the things Andy liked best about Sue.

Mr. Sato looked at his watch and said something quietly to his wife. Andy realized that time was passing, and that the concert would be starting in a little more than an hour. The usual preconcert fluttering in his stomach began, and suddenly the sight of the elegant dinner nauseated him. It was time to get moving.

When Sue arrived at the Kasei School, she found Haruko talking to Andy for a change, instead of standing with Mia, Ginny, and the other "real" American kids.

"Hey, Sue," Andy greeted her. "Ready for the concert?"

Sue saw that his shoulders looked stiff and his hand was tightly clenched on the handle of his violin case. He was suffering from his usual preconcert jitters. Sue wanted to put her arms around him and comfort him, but that would embarrass him in front of the others. Instead, she gave him a big grin and said, "Of course I am! I don't think you have to worry, either. Anybody who can catch goldfish with a paper scoop shouldn't have trouble with a violin solo!"

After a second Andy laughed, and his shoulders relaxed. The others wanted to know about the goldfish, and Sue gave them an exaggerated account of Andy's heroically going after the goldfish with his paper scoop.

"All right, folks," Mr. Baxter said. "Let's show them!"

"See you later, Andy," said Haruko as she joined the

other Japanese kids heading for the entrance of the auditorium.

Sue thought Haruko gave Andy a significant look before she left. "She seems a lot friendlier than she was before," she remarked to Andy as they were lining up behind the curtains.

"Apparently my so-called heroics in the pachinko parlor made quite an impression on her family," said Andy.

Sue felt her chest tightening. "What exactly did her family do?" she asked, as casually as she could manage.

"Would you believe it, they started asking about my background!" said Andy, laughing. "For a while I thought they were looking me over as a potential son-in-law!"

The tightness in Sue's chest became painful. "So what happened?"

Andy grinned. "When I told them my ancestors were farmers, not samurai, they gave up on me."

"I thought you were interested in Haruko," said Sue. "You were working so hard to impress her."

Andy looked down at Sue, and his face became serious again. "Sue, I was never interested in her. The thing is, I can't resist a challenge. When I saw her sneering at me, I promised myself that I would make her respect me."

"And she does respect you, after that yakuza business," Sue said in a low voice. "You can be friends with her now."

She felt Andy's arms go around her. "Sue, don't tell me you're jealous of Haruko?" he said in her ear. "Come on, you should know by now I'm crazy about you!"

"But you and Haruko share an ancestry," said Sue, afraid to let herself be comforted. "You seem to have so much in common with her. Things I could never understand."

Andy laughed softly. "After all we've been through with your parents and my parents, I thought we've agreed that ancestry doesn't matter. To us, anyway. You know, I'm getting awfully homesick."

"I'm homesick, too," whispered Sue.

"Hey, better line up, everybody!" said Mr. Baxter. "We're getting ready to go on!"

The players began to shuffle around, moving into their own sections of the orchestra. Andy squeezed Sue's hand as they parted ways and Sue joined the viola players. She exchanged smiles with her stand partner.

When they finally walked onstage and took their places, they had to sit quietly while speeches were made. First, the principal of the Kasei School gave a long speech in Japanese. Another long speech, also in Japanese, was made by the conductor of the Kasei orchestra. Sue guessed that he was telling some funny stories about their visit to the U.S., since there were bursts of laughter from the audience.

Then it was Mr. Baxter's turn to speak. He had the sense to keep his speech short, knowing that not all the audience understood English. Besides, he knew that his players were fidgeting impatiently, waiting to start the concert.

At last, Mr. Baxter finished with some graceful words of thanks to the school for their invitation. The applause continued as he turned around and faced the orchestra. He gave them a nod and raised his baton.

Their opening number was Schubert's Rosamunde Overture. The orchestra members got over their nervousness, and in the faster sections, they managed to bring out the humor in the piece. The audience applauded vigorously.

Then came the Bach concerto. Sue's heart began to beat fast as she saw Andy and his fellow soloist walk to the front of the stage. Andy's face was somber, and Sue could tell he was suffering from a bad case of stage fright.

A solo was always a test of the player's nerve. Sue knew that even when Andy played a solo in the Lakeview auditorium, he felt the pressure. Now the pressure was much more intense. Andy had to prove himself in the country of his ancestors. Everybody in the audience had probably noticed that his name was Suzuki, and would be expecting a lot from him.

During the opening section of the concerto, Sue was too busy with her own part to look at Andy. When the orchestra stopped for the entrance of the soloists, Sue turned to look at Andy again. The concertmaster had the first solo, and while he was playing, Andy relaxed slightly. By the time it was his turn, he was able to smile and bring his bow down decisively. The first movement, full of bouncy rhythm, went well.

The second movement was the real test, however. It opened with a long, lyrical passage by the second soloist, which was Andy's part. When the conductor raised his baton, Sue saw that Andy was gripping his bow so hard that his knuckles were white. If his nervousness made his playing shaky, the whole audience would sense his discomfort. It would ruin the movement. It would ruin the concerto. It might ruin the whole concert.

Sue saw Andy close his eyes and take a deep breath. A sense of peace seemed to come over him. His notes, when he finally played them, were soft at first, then gradually increased in volume. They had a melting beauty that came from absolute serenity.

Somehow, Andy had found in Japan the serenity that helped him overcome his fears.

the next morning, the Chongs took Sue back to Narita Airport by express train. As the scenery whizzed by, they talked about Sue's experiences during her visit to Japan. She mentioned unforgettable sights, like her first view of the huge lanterns at the Asakusa Temple and the peaceful face of the Great Buddha in Kamakura. She also mentioned less pleasant things, like the suffocating heat, the humidity, and the crowds in the buses and subways. She even told the Chongs about the scary encounter with the yakuza in the pachinko parlor.

Mrs. Chong nodded solemnly. "So, overall, what is your impression of Japan and the Japanese people?" she asked Sue.

"Um, I don't know what I can say after only five days here!" said Sue. She didn't feel comfortable making a general statement about the Japanese people. From the way her mother felt about the Japanese—and the way Andy's father felt about the Chinese—Sue knew how dangerous it was to stereotype people.

"Well, surely you can tell me how you were treated by the Japanese," said Mrs. Chong. "Did you feel discriminated against because you are Chinese?"

Sue thought over her experiences. "Well, I don't think they could tell that I'm Chinese," she said honestly. "I look like I could be Japanese, until I speak. And then I sound American." Then she thought of Haruko, who *did* know she was Chinese American. "Actually, Haruko Sato—you took me to her house, you know—was much nicer to *me* than to *Andy*. And he's Japanese American."

Mrs. Chong looked thoughtful. Finally she said, "Perhaps that's because you're a guest in her country, not someone who lives here. The Japanese are always very kind to guests."

Sue remembered how in the pachinko parlor, the yakuza had stopped bullying them when he learned that she was a guest from America. She couldn't imagine gang members in America being that polite to people just because they were guests. "Then why was Haruko so mean to Andy?" she asked. "He's a guest, too."

"Maybe she feels that he's really Japanese," Mrs. Chong speculated. "So she thinks he ought to behave like a proper Japanese boy. That would explain why she's so unforgiving whenever he makes a mistake."

Sue frowned. "The Japanese discriminate against

you," she pointed out. "Aren't you guests—even though your family came as unwilling guests?"

It was Mr. Chong who answered. "We're here permanently, you see. That makes us no longer guests, only a nuisance."

"They feel the same way about the Chinese who come here looking for work," added Mrs. Chong. "They are no longer guests, either. Don't Americans discriminate against immigrants from poor countries who go there looking for jobs?"

"I guess you're right," Sue admitted. What she did not say was that immigrants who adapted to life in America eventually became accepted by most Americans, even if it took a while. Her own family was an example of that.

Sue remembered the strips on the sidewalks where blind people could feel their way. She also thought of the music played at intersections. "I was impressed by how considerate the Japanese are to the handicapped," she remarked to the Chongs. "You can hear tunes played at busy intersections downtown so a blind person can tell which street has the green light."

"It's not considerate if your handicaps include having a terrible ear," said Mrs. Chong. They laughed. "The Japanese do show a lot of compassion toward the weak and the handicapped," agreed Mrs. Chong.

Sue thought of the teenage boy holding a parasol over his grandmother. "They're very considerate of the elderly here, too. In America, a lot of the elderly are stashed away in retirement communities or nursing homes. My friend Andy tells me that at the Satos', the elderly grandfather is staying with them."

"There is respect for the elderly in most Asian cultures, I think," said Mr. Chong. "You also have that among the Chinese, don't you?"

Sue nodded. "Especially respect for old women. Some old women in China can be pretty tough." She thought of Grandma Mei. "In fact, I'm a little scared of facing my grandmother when I go home. She's mad at me because my boyfriend's family is from Japan."

Mrs. Chong looked curiously at Sue. "Tell me if I'm being offensive, but as a Chinese, don't you feel uncomfortable having a Japanese boyfriend?"

"Andy thinks of himself as Japanese American," said Sue. "Anyway, when you really get to know someone, you forget who his ancestors are. He's just a person."

"It's easy to forget if you haven't suffered," murmured Mr. Chong. "Here in Tokyo, we still get reminders that we are Korean."

"My grandmother did suffer at the hands of the Japanese soldiers," admitted Sue, remembering Grandma Mei's implacable face. "And it's true that she hasn't forgotten."

Sue wondered why it seemed much harder in Japan to blend into the mainstream culture. "I guess who your ancestors are is still very important in Japan," she said. "In America, your ancestors don't matter so much. You're just *you*. But in Japan, if your ancestors tanned leather hundreds of years ago or were samurai, you're still affected by that now."

Mrs. Chong nodded. "But you are still somewhat

affected by your ancestry in America, aren't you? You preserve parts of the Chinese culture in your life. You honor what your grandmother went through."

Sue nodded. "*Honor.* I guess that's the thing. I want to honor my grandmother's life but still live my own, you know?"

Mrs. Chong smiled. "You seem like a very bright girl, Sue. I'm sure you'll find your way." She turned to look out the window, leaving Sue with her own thoughts. *Find my own way. How can I explain that to Grandma Mei?*

Suddenly Sue was impatient to get home, home to America. The train began to slow down as it approached Narita Airport, and Sue could hardly stay in her seat. She didn't know how she would be able to stand the long flight back.

But at the same time, she felt a pang at leaving new friends like the Chongs, and even Haruko. Also, there was so much more to see. Just comparing experiences with the other Lakeview kids made her realize that she had barely skimmed the surface of Tokyo. *And there's all the rest of Japan, too. I'll have to come back someday—with Andy, maybe?*

Then she had another idea. Maybe someday she and Andy could visit China together! It would be a visit of self-discovery for her, just as the Tokyo trip had been a visit of self-discovery for Andy. She would be showing Andy what sort of people she came from. And she was sure that, like Andy, she would also find out how much she differed from her ancestors.

* * *

"Ladies and gentlemen, the plane will be landing in twenty minutes. Please fasten your seat belts, put back your tray tables, and make sure your seats are in the up-right position. The flight attendants will come by for your headsets and any remaining items to be discarded."

Sue yawned and adjusted her seat. She had taken a couple of short naps, but she still wanted to sleep uninterrupted for about a week when she got home.

She looked at Andy, who was awake and trying to work a crossword puzzle from the in-flight magazine. "What's a three-letter word for 'cuckoo'?" he asked. He looked pretty groggy.

Personally, Sue felt that he should have taken a nap, instead of watching all those movies shown after their meals. "I don't know a three-letter word for 'cuckoo,' " she said. "In fact, I don't know of any word for 'cuckoo' other than 'cuckoo.' "

Andy smiled at her. He reached over and pushed her hair out of her eyes, and Sue settled her head lightly on his shoulder. The attendant came around collecting cans, cups, and other trash. Sue could feel the plane swoop and make dips as it circled to land. Now that they were almost home, her sleepiness disappeared and she was starting to feel excited. She thought about how much she had missed her parents and Rochelle. She had missed Grandma Mei a lot, too, although she knew she would still have to face her grandmother's anger over Andy.

Andy put the magazine back in the seat pocket, straightened his chair, and looked fixedly ahead. Sue realized that he was tense.

Sue put her hand on his. "Why are you so uptight? You know you did great in the concert. You can relax now."

Andy took a deep breath, and Sue could see his visible effort to be calm. Finally he seemed to succeed. "I guess I was thinking about what I should tell my dad about the trip."

"What's so hard about that?" asked Sue, puzzled. "Just tell him what happened."

"But it was such a mess!" said Andy, beginning to sound edgy again. "He'll want a neat summary of how I found my roots, how I responded to the exposure to my ancestral culture, and so on. The trouble is, all I can remember are stupid things like pachinko parlors and catching goldfish with a paper scoop!"

Sue laughed. She had met Mr. Suzuki only briefly at the parents' meetings, and she didn't think he would subject Andy to an examination. Her own father, being a professor, was more likely to do that. Or Grandma Mei. "You're luckier than I am," she told Andy. "I have to make a report to my grandmother, who will want to know about all the Japanese monsters I met."

For some weird reason, the mention of Grandma Mei seemed to cheer Andy up. He smiled at Sue and leaned back in his seat as the plane descended and touched the tarmac.

Passing through immigration, waiting for their luggage, and going through customs seemed to take forever. But at last they were out. They were home!

Sue spotted her parents and Rochelle right away. Grandma Mei wasn't with them. Sue wasn't sure whether that was a good thing. She ran up and was immediately engulfed in hugs and kisses. All around her, she heard cries as the other players greeted their families. When the hysterical welcomes died down a bit, they began to make their way to the parking garage.

Sue looked around for Andy. Where was he? To her surprise, she saw that he and his parents were walking right behind her family. She was even more surprised when her mother stopped and waved to Mr. and Mrs. Suzuki. "Don't forget to tell your son that we're expecting him for dinner tomorrow night."

Sue could hardly believe her ears. Her *mother* was inviting Andy? Her mother, the Japanese hater? "A lot must have happened while I was away," she said when they reached their car.

Sue's mother smiled at her astonishment. "You remember we met the Suzukis at the airport coffee shop when we were seeing you off?"

Of course Sue hadn't forgotten. Nor had she forgotten Grandma Mei's fury when she discovered that she had actually shared a table with a Japanese family. "So what happened after we boarded the plane?" Sue asked.

Rochelle was the one who answered. "You should have heard the fireworks! Grandma Mei accused us of setting up the whole thing, to make her eat with the Suzukis!"

"Did you convince her that we didn't plan it?" asked Sue.

Rochelle laughed. "Dad was the one who finally convinced Grandma that it wasn't a big plot, and that we met the Suzukis entirely by accident."

Sue turned gratefully to her father. "Thanks, Dad!" She knew her father was the person Grandma Mei respected the most. He was the only one who could calm her grandmother's fury.

After they got home from the airport, Rochelle filled Sue in on what had happened. "Next day Dad called Mr. Suzuki to apologize for Grandma Mei's freak-out at the airport."

"What did Mr. Suzuki say?" asked Sue nervously. She suddenly remembered what Andy had told her about the bad experiences his father had had in China.

"He said he had already forgotten about it," said Rochelle. She winked. "Mr. Suzuki went on to say how much he admired Mom's artwork, and he wanted to know whether she was doing more landscape paintings."

Sue winked back. "Ohhh, that explains it. I was wondering why Mom is suddenly feeling so friendly toward the Suzukis."

Sue's alarm clock woke her up at ten o'clock the next morning. She could easily have gone back to sleep, but she struggled up, determined to get adjusted to local time as quickly as possible.

She spent the day in a fog. She did her laundry and chatted with Rochelle about Japan. She handed out some souvenirs she had bought in Tokyo. For her mother she had bought a shopping bag decorated with an aborigine Ainu design, for her father a primitive woodblock print, and for Rochelle a brocade fan. She had a similar fan for Grandma Mei.

Sue almost forgot that Andy was coming over for dinner until she saw her mother starting to prepare the meal.

"Why so much food, Mom?" Sue asked as she helped chop vegetables. "Believe me, Andy's no gourmet. He'd be happy with some sandwiches and chips."

"Andy is not the only guest joining us for dinner this evening," Sue's mom replied, looking up from her cooking to wink at Sue. "Grandma Mei will also be joining us. I thought it would be nice for us to all sit down and get to know one another."

Sue slowly turned back to her vegetables. "Uh . . . great." But she wasn't so convinced it was great. *Isn't that just asking for trouble? And what if Grandma Mei's still mad at me?*

"Mom, does Grandma know that Andy will be here?" Sue asked.

Her mother grinned. "No. Let's give her a big surprise!"

"Oh, sure, she will just love your big surprise," muttered Sue.

Her mother's face became serious. "Listen, Sue, Grandma Mei wasn't angry just because your boyfriend is Japanese. What hurt her the most was the fact that you kept this a secret. That's why I want Andy to come here openly and face Grandma."

Sue knew her mother was right, but that didn't make the waiting any easier.

Half an hour later, Grandma Mei arrived. Sue didn't wait to see whether her grandmother was still angry with her or not. She ran up, hugged her grandmother hard, and gave her the fan. "See, Grandma, I got back safe and sound."

Before her grandmother could reply, the bell rang again. Andy stood at the door, dressed in his dark suit, white shirt, and tie. Sue smiled in spite of herself. He looked good enough to eat, but when he saw Grandma Mei, he stopped dead and swallowed.

Grandma Mei stared at Andy with no expression at all. Sue waited for the fireworks to start.

Andy took a deep breath. With shaking hands, he brought out a package from behind his back and handed it to Grandma Mei. "I bought this especially for you, Mrs. Mei."

"Open it, Mother," said Sue's mother, and everybody joined in urging her to open the package.

"Yes, let's see what Andy's brought," urged Sue's father.

Sue tried to catch Andy's eye and give him a "What's this?" look, but Andy wouldn't take his eyes off Grandma Mei. Sue remembered the package he'd had at the Chinese store. Did that have something to do with this surprise gift?

Slowly, Grandma Mei tore open the colorful wrapping paper and then the flimsy tissue paper. Everyone leaned in to see the contents. Inside was a doll dressed in an elegant Chinese brocade jacket with a high collar and buttons down the sides, and trousers of shiny silk. Grandma Mei stared wordlessly at the doll, and then looked up at Andy.

The doll! The doll the Japanese soldiers destroyed. He

remembered! Sue ached to reach over and give Andy a hug, but she was waiting to see how Grandma Mei would react.

Andy cleared his throat. "I know that you lost your doll when those Japanese soldiers broke into your home. This is to make up for their actions."

"Andy, your family had nothing to do with those soldiers!" Sue cried. "Your grandparents were in America at the time. In fact, your grandfather even joined the U.S. Army and served in Italy!"

"But I still offer my apology for the actions of the soldiers," said Andy. "I hope you will accept it."

Grandma Mei stared at the doll, and then she did the last thing they expected. She burst out into gales of laughter.

"This . . . this isn't . . . isn't . . . at all like the doll I lost. That was just a crude clay doll, wearing a cotton jacket!"

Andy looked nervous. "Shall I exchange the doll?" he asked.

Grandma Mei looked at Andy and then back at the doll. Suddenly she bent over. This time she was not laughing. She was sobbing.

Sue went over and put her arms around her grandmother. "Andy meant well, Grandma."

Grandma Mei wiped her eyes and nodded. Cradling the doll, she turned to Andy. "Thank you," she said huskily. "You're right: the war is over."

Sue raised her head and her eyes met Andy's. She had been attracted to him because he was good-looking, because he was a wonderful violinist, and because the two of them enjoyed the same kind of humor. In buying the doll for Grandma Mei, he showed another side of himself, a side that touched her deeply.

Well done, Andy, Sue mouthed silently. Andy smiled at her.

The past is done and the war is over. Sue walked over and squeezed Andy's hand. *Now we can start to think about the future.*

about the author

lensey Namioka was born in Beijing and moved to the United States when she was a child. She is the author of many books for young people, including *Ties That Bind, Ties That Break,* an ALA Top Ten Book for Young Adults, and its companion novel, *An Ocean Apart, a World Away.* Her middle-grade novels include *Half and Half; Yang the Youngest and His Terrible Ear,* a Young Reader's Choice Award nominee; *Yang the Third and Her Impossible Family; Yang the Second and Her Secret Admirers; Yang the Eldest and His Odd Jobs;* and *April and the Dragon Lady,* a nominee for the Utah Young Adults' Book Award. Several of Lensey Namioka's beloved Samurai mysteries have recently come back into print: *The Samurai and the Long-Nosed Devils, White Serpent Castle, Valley of the Broken Cherry Trees,* and *Village of the Vampire Cat.* Lensey Namioka lives in Seattle with her family.